Topz SECRET STORIES

DANNY AND THE RUNAWAY

Alexa Tewkesbury

CWR

Hi there!
I'm Rick - I'm in the Dixons Gang.

You might have heard of us. There's me and my mates, Clyde and Kevin, and we all live on the Dixons Estate, in Holly Hill.

There's not that much to do in Holly Hill so we like to hang out together. The best places are the shopping centre and the park – there's lots of room there to play football or ride a bike.

Sometimes we run into the Topz Gang. 'Topzies' we call them just cos it bugs them. They're really annoying – they always seem to be talking about God and I don't get it. Us Dixons, we're cool. But Topz, they're just a waste of space.

Now my friend Lily is coming to stay with us. She's all right, I guess, but I've a feeling there's something she's not telling me.

That's what this story is all about ...

Hi! We're the Topz Gang –

Topz because we all live at the 'top' of something …
either in houses at the top of the hill, at the top of the
flats by the park, even sleeping in a top bunk counts!

We are all Christians, and we go to Holly Hill School.

We love Jesus, and try to work out our faith in God
in everything we do – at home, at school and with our
friends. That even means trying to show God's love to
the Dixons Gang who tend to be bullies, and can be a
real pain!

If you'd like to know more about us, visit our website
at www.cwr.org.uk/topz. You can read all about us,
and how you can get to know and understand the Bible
more by reading our *Topz* notes, which are great fun,
and written every two months just for you!

One

'You know you can still come with us, Lily. It's not too late. You don't have to stay here on your own.'

Denise had lost count of the number of times she'd invited her daughter to go away with her and Andy on their honeymoon. It felt as if they'd had the same conversation over and over.

'*Why* won't you come, Lily?' Denise would ask.

'It's your honeymoon, Mum,' Lily would shrug. 'No one takes their kid with them on their honeymoon.'

'But it's not really a honeymoon, is it? I know we're getting married but it's just a little holiday, that's all.'

'Not *that* little. You're going away for a whole month.'

'Yes, I know.' Denise sounded a little more tired each time they talked about it. 'And that's why we'd like you to come with us. Andy loves you, you know he does. I love you, too. I don't want to be away from you for a month.'

'So why are you going?'

'Because, Lily, Andy is going to be my husband and as you know perfectly well he has family in New Zealand whom he really wants me to meet. He'd like you to meet them, too, but you're obviously going to carry on being silly and difficult about it. Why do you have to be such a puzzle? Let's just forget it, shall we? I shan't ask you again.'

Of course, Denise did ask again. She couldn't help it. She felt that a month away from Holly Hill all together, somewhere fresh and exciting, would do them a whole world of good. It would help them to feel they belonged to each other; cement them together as a new family of three.

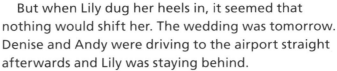

But when Lily dug her heels in, it seemed that nothing would shift her. The wedding was tomorrow. Denise and Andy were driving to the airport straight afterwards and Lily was staying behind.

'They say they want me to go with them, but they don't,' she'd said matter-of-factly to her friend, Rick, one day. 'It's obvious they just want to be with each other. Anyway, why would I want to hang around with *them*? They're all, "Oh, I love you so much, darling dinky-donks!" all the time. Makes me feel sick.'

Rick threw her a sideways glance. 'Dinky-donks?' he frowned.

'Well, words like that anyway,' answered Lily. 'They're always calling each other some silly name or other.'

'Sounds a bit rubbish.'

'It is. You're so lucky it's just you and the twins and your mum. Don't *ever* let her get a boyfriend. It'll ruin your life.'

Rick wasn't normally one for getting involved in other people's troubles. He was one of the Dixons Gang – three boys from the Dixons Estate who always seemed happier *causing* trouble than trying to sort it out. But Rick had known Lily a long time. Lily's mum, Denise, was his own mum's best friend. Denise was also his mum's hairdresser. When it was time for a wash and cut, Rick was always left in charge of his little twin sisters, Naomi and Alesha, while the two mums chatted and chatted – and then chatted some more.

Lately, the chat had been all about how lucky Denise was to have found a lovely man like Andy; how the wedding preparations were going; how Denise couldn't wait to be flying off to New Zealand with her new husband, but how it was breaking her heart that Lily wasn't going with them.

'I don't know what to do,' Denise had said a few weeks before, as she snipped away at Rick's mum's hair. 'Lily just refuses to come with us. I mean, she can go and stay with my sister but that's a good couple of hours away from here so she won't be able to get to school. If she was coming to New Zealand I could arrange for her to have the time off, but if she's staying here she ought to be going in every day as normal. In any case, my sister's out working and Lily can't be left at home all day every day on her own.'

'Well …' Rick's mum, Elaine, chewed her lip thoughtfully. 'If you're really stuck, Denise, Lily can come here.'

Denise smiled, but shook her head. 'No, I couldn't possibly ask you to do that.'

'You're *not* asking, though, are you?' Elaine replied. 'I've offered.'

'Yes, but you've already got three kids to look after. I'm quite sure you don't need another one. Besides, where's she going to sleep?'

'Rick can bunk in with his little sisters. They'll love it! Or he can sleep downstairs. Then Lily can have *his* room.'

'I can't see Rick liking the sound of that very much,' said Denise, shaking her head again.

'Oh, he won't mind,' Elaine replied. 'He's a good boy really. And he likes your Lily. Anyway, it's only for a month. Be nice having her around for a bit. We can have girlie chats. Naomi and Alesha are a bit too small for that yet.'

Denise still looked doubtful. 'That's such a kind offer,' she murmured hesitantly. 'Just seems like a lot of extra work for you. I'll have a think. In any case,' she added, brightening, 'by the time the wedding comes round,

Lily'll probably have changed her mind and be coming to New Zealand with us.'

'Let's hope so, eh?' Rick's mum nodded. 'But if the worst comes to the worst, at least you know she's welcome here.'

Now it seemed that the worst *had* come. Reluctantly, Denise started to help Lily pack up her things; her clothes and games and books. But they weren't packing another suitcase for New Zealand. They were getting ready for Lily to go and stay with Rick and his family.

'You know you can't take much,' Denise fussed. 'Rick's bedroom's stuffed to the eyeballs as it is. It's so kind of Elaine to have you but, honestly, I just don't see how she's got the space.'

'It'll be fine,' Lily muttered. She rolled up her dressing gown and jammed it into the case. 'I don't want to take much anyway.'

'Well, I'll leave a house key with Elaine. Then at least if you find you haven't got something you need, you can pop back home and pick it up.'

'I won't need anything,' was all Lily replied.

Late that afternoon, Lily and her mum stood either side of the suitcase and two carrier bags on Elaine's doorstep. Denise didn't ring the bell straight away.

'Please come back and stay at home tonight, Lily,' she said quietly.

'No, that's OK.' Lily shook her head. 'All my stuff's packed now so I may as well stay here. Besides, Auntie Mandy's coming and you'll be up half the night talking. You said she wants to do lots of messing about with your hair and makeup. I'll just be in the way.'

'Of course you won't be in the way!' Denise answered. 'It's my wedding day tomorrow, Lil. You can both help me get ready. It'll be exciting.'

'No, honestly, Mum. I'll be fine here.'

Wedding day excitement was something Lily could do without. As far as she was concerned, staying at Rick's the night before was the perfect escape plan.

The moment Lily was in the house, Rick's twin sisters, Naomi and Alesha, rushed at her.

'Lily!' Alesha shrieked, delighted that their guest had arrived. 'Come up to our room. We can play something.'

'You can play with me, too, Lily,' piped Naomi. 'We can all play together.'

'Calm down, you two,' Elaine interrupted firmly. 'Lily's just walked in the door. Leave her alone for five minutes at least.'

'Can we play after five minutes, then?' Naomi persisted.

'I'm sure Lily will play with you when she feels like it,' Elaine replied. 'But for now she needs to get herself unpacked and settled in, so just leave her alone.' Then, 'Rick!' she called over her shoulder. 'Go upstairs with Lily and show her where she can put her stuff, will you?'

In his bedroom, Rick pulled open the two top drawers in the chest in the corner.

'You can use those, if you like,' he said. 'Mum told me to clear them out.'

'You didn't have to,' Lily answered.

'There's a bit of space in the cupboard, too.'

Lily hesitated. 'Are you sure you're OK about this, Rick? I don't mind sleeping in with the twins.'

'I'm not really bothered,' Rick shrugged. 'It's only for a month, isn't it? Anyway, I'm out a lot.'

Lily nodded. 'Just as long as you're sure.'

'I said so, didn't I?' Rick looked a little uncomfortable as he hovered in the doorway. 'Anyway, I'll let you get sorted. Come down when you're ready. And Alesha and Naomi can be really annoying so if you want them to leave you alone, just tell them.'

Lily smiled. Then Rick was gone and she was left standing, suitcase and bags still grasped in her hands, looking at the closed bedroom door. It was another few moments before she dropped them to the floor.

She sat down on the end of Rick's bed and her eyes flicked around the room. She'd been in here several times before, but it looked different now. It was much tidier than usual, but that wasn't it. The difference was that now she'd be sleeping here; doing homework here. Living here. This would be her space for the next month. The thin curtains and grey carpet were what she'd be waking up to every morning. Her mum would be on the other side of the world and even when she came home, nothing would ever be the same again.

That's when Lily's body shuddered and the tears came. They spilled down her cheeks and she didn't try to stop them. She sat still on the bed and sobbed silently. As if she was all alone. It was only when Elaine's voice called up the stairs that she seemed to remember where she was.

'Are you all right, Lily? Do you need any help?'

'Erm ...' Lily hastily wiped her face with her hands scrunched into fists. 'I'm fine,' she gulped. 'I'll be down in a sec.'

'No hurry, darling,' Elaine replied. 'Just let me know if there's anything you want.'

Lily sniffed hard and rubbed at her nose. If only it was that simple, she thought.

There was only one thing Lily wanted. She wanted to go back to life before Andy.

Lily had never known her real dad. He'd gone before she was born. For her whole life it had been just Lily and her mum. They were more like best friends than mother and daughter. They'd eat chocolate ice cream together while they watched TV. They'd do each other's hair. They'd go shopping and pick out outfits for each other. Their life together had been perfect. Better than perfect.

But now that her mum was getting married, that perfection made it all the harder to let go.

It wasn't that Lily didn't like Andy. Somewhere inside herself she knew she did. He was kind. He was nice to her. He could even make her laugh out loud with his silly jokes. And there was no doubt that he made her mum very happy.

But that didn't change the fact that everything was different now. Lily had never known what it was like to have a dad, and she'd certainly never wanted or needed a stepdad. All she wanted was her mum. All she needed was her mum's love.

As far as Lily was concerned, whatever went on in the future, one thing was for sure: **Andy would always come between them.**

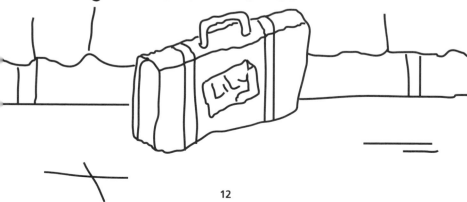

Two

Danny wasn't talking. He hadn't said a word since he'd mumbled, 'Bye, Dad,' on the station platform a few hours earlier. He'd stood beside his mum while his dad waved at them from his seat next to the window. Then they'd watched the train pull away and rumble off into the distance. They'd kept watching until they couldn't see it any more.

'He'll be back before you know it,' Danny's mum said softly. 'I mean I know it'll only be for odd weekends for a while, but he *will* be back, I promise. Anyway, might be quite nice having the place to ourselves,' she added, peering into Danny's face. Hoping to get a smile.

Danny didn't look at her. He continued to stare stony-faced at the now empty railway line. He knew his mum was trying to be brave. He knew he should give her a hug or at least say something to try to cheer her up. His dad going away was hard on her, too.

But he didn't. He kept his hands stuffed in his pockets and he wouldn't say a word. This shouldn't be happening. It was all wrong. His dad belonged at home. They needed him.

The trouble was they needed money, too. His dad had recently lost his job so he'd had to look for work anywhere he could find it. Danny understood that – but couldn't the 'anywhere' at least have been in England? After four long months of filling in application forms and going to interviews, with no job offers from any of them, Danny's uncle rang. Would his dad be interested in a manager's post with the company he ran in Spain? Spain!

Of course his dad had said yes. He didn't want to leave Holly Hill. He most certainly didn't want to leave his family. But he desperately needed a job. So what else *could* he say?

When Danny told his friends in the Topz Gang, Benny's first thought was, 'But that's *so* cool, Danny! That's where Spanish omelettes come from!'

Danny blinked at him. '*What?*'

'Omelettes,' Benny repeated. 'Spanish ones. That's where they come from.'

'Is it?' Danny looked even more confused.

'It must be,' insisted Benny. 'That's why they're called *Spanish* omelettes.'

Paul, another member of the Gang, peered at Benny over the top of his glasses. 'So, what's the difference between a Spanish omelette and an English omelette?' he asked.

'Easy,' answered Benny. 'A Spanish omelette's got potato in it.'

'Can't you put potato in an English omelette?'

'No, Paul, because then it wouldn't be English, would it? It'd be Spanish.'

Danny leapt to his feet. 'Why are we talking about omelettes?' he snapped. 'Didn't any of you hear what I said? My dad's got to go and work in Spain. Which means he's going to have to live there for most of the time. Which also means I'll hardly ever see him. So who *cares* what kind of omelettes you get in Spain, Benny? I'm losing my dad!'

What made it even harder for Danny was that he'd been asking God to find his dad a job in Holly Hill. He'd prayed every day. Danny couldn't understand why the days and weeks and months were passing with his dad still out of work, but he didn't give up. He kept talking to God. He kept asking Him. He never once stopped trusting that God would sort it out. It just might take time.

Then one day his dad announced that he was going to Spain. And Danny felt as if his heart had fallen out of his chest and hit the floor.

He didn't wait to hear about the job. He didn't care what it was his dad would have to do or when he might be leaving to make a start. He stormed to his room, slammed the door shut behind him and threw himself onto his bed.

Why, God?
He asked it over and over again.

You're supposed to work things out for the best. That's Your promise, God. That's the promise I've been trusting in. So why is Dad going to Spain? Why didn't You find him a job here? WHY?

A few weeks went by, full of preparations and arrangements, packing and even more form-filling. Every day, Danny hoped the situation would change. He prayed that his dad would find another job in England; even in Holly Hill.

He didn't.

And suddenly it was time to say goodbye.

When Danny and his mum got back from the station, Danny went straight to his bedroom.

'Denise is coming soon to cut my hair,' he heard his mum say outside his door. 'Come and say hello when she gets here, will you, Danny?'

Danny didn't answer. Why should he? His stomach was twisted in a tight knot. He felt as though he'd been emptied out. All he could see was the mile upon mile of railway line and road and sea that would now separate him from his dad.

So maybe he wouldn't speak at all, not to anyone, until his dad came home again. How long could he go on not speaking, he wondered, before his voice stopped working?

He reached across to his bedside table and picked up his Bible. There was a postcard sticking out and he flipped the pages over to the one the card marked. His eyes fell instantly on the verse he wanted to remember:

'We know that in all things God works for good with those who love him ...' (Romans 8:28).

Danny didn't need to read it to remember it. He knew it so well he could even say it backwards. But it helped to see it written there. That's when he knew it wasn't something he had made up or imagined. This was God's Word. God's promise. If you loved God and trusted Him, He would do what was best for you – Danny was convinced of that.

Danny's mum and dad didn't know God yet. That was something else Danny kept praying for. They asked lots of questions. They sometimes went to church with him. But they hadn't quite given their lives over to God. They still needed to realise that He loved them; that being friends with Him was the best thing ever.

But Danny loved God. He talked to Him about everything. He knew that God listened to him and he knew God understood and loved him too. That's why it was so hard to believe that He had allowed his family to be split up. If this was God's idea of working something out in the best way, Danny couldn't make it out.

Yet still he read the verse: *'... in all things God works for good with those who love him ...'* He kept on reading it, because deep inside he knew that God wouldn't let him down. God must be doing something. He *must* be.

The doorbell rang. Denise had arrived. Danny's mum wasn't likely to ask him to come and say hello again. She hardly ever asked him more than once to do anything. Today she knew how upset he was, so whatever she asked, she probably didn't expect him to do it.

Slowly, Danny closed his Bible. He had a choice. Start talking or stay silent for the next month or so until his dad came home for a visit. In which case, how would he even be able to speak to his dad on the phone when he rang later to say he'd arrived?

'... *God works for good ...*'

Danny knew he was being silly. He needed to talk. Everyone needs to talk.

Outside the kitchen, he paused. His mum was chuckling about something. That was a good sign.

'I meant what I said, Denise. You really didn't have to bother with my hair today. You should be thinking about yourself. You're the one who's getting married tomorrow.'

'It's no trouble, is it?' Denise replied. 'Andy's at work and Lily's off swimming. Everything's organised so what else would I be doing? Worrying that the day's going to go all right? Worrying that the food's going to taste all right? Worrying that I'm going to *look* all right! I could drive myself mad with worry if I was at home on my own right now. Besides,' she added, 'I don't want my friends turning up at my wedding with their hair in a mess. I've got the photos to think about!'

The two of them burst out laughing.

'Let me put the kettle on,' said Danny's mum. 'Sounds like we could both do with a cuppa. I mean, here I am, Denise, without my husband because he's heading off to work in another country – and there you are about to get yourself a brand-new one!'

'I know!' It sounded to Danny as though Denise was still smiling. 'Crazy, isn't it? But ...' She hesitated. 'Well, you didn't really have a choice, did you? Taking the job had to be the number one priority. For now, at least. But, Andy and me? This is *my choice*, isn't it? He asked me to marry him and I said yes. I thought it was for the best. For Lily as well as for me. But now I'm not so sure. I really felt she'd have come round to the idea after all this time. I thought she'd want to help me with the planning; choosing the dress, the flowers … everything. I thought she'd be as excited as me. Honestly, I've been like a big kid with it all! Not Lily, though. She's really had nothing to do with any of it. I'm getting married tomorrow and she's not even going to be my bridesmaid.'

'And she's still not going to New Zealand with you?' Danny's mum asked.

'No. She's going to stay with her friend on the Dixons Estate,' Denise replied.

'Oh, who's that?'

'Do you know Rick? He's in her class at Southlands School. His mum's a good friend of mine. Elaine. A very good friend as it turns out. I don't know where else Lily could have gone for a whole month. I'm dropping her round there later so she can get settled in.'

Outside the kitchen door, Danny frowned. Rick from the Dixons Estate? Did Denise mean Rick from the Dixons Gang? Poor Lily. That didn't sound like a very good idea. It wasn't just that Topz and Dixons didn't get on. No one seemed to get on with Dixons. A lot of the kids around Holly Hill were scared of them. Dixons liked it that way. It meant they could be kings of the park; kings of the shopping centre. Kings of Holly Hill.

You didn't stand up to a gang like Dixons.

'Anyway,' sighed Denise. 'Enough about me. How are you? And what about your Danny now his dad's actually gone?'

Danny didn't give his mum a chance to answer. He pushed the door open and walked into the kitchen.

'I'm all right,' he said. 'Just got to get used to it, I suppose.'

He glanced at his mum. She smiled at him.

'It's going to be a bit of a shock to the system for a while,' his mum added, still looking at him. 'But we'll be all right, won't we, Danny? We can talk to Dad on the computer. We've got that thing sorted out where you can see each other while you're chatting. It'll be like watching him on TV, won't it, Danny?'

'It's such a shame he had to leave before the wedding,' said Denise.

'I know,' nodded Danny's mum. 'He was ever so disappointed.'

'But you'll still both be there, won't you?' Denise glanced from one to the other.

Again, Danny felt his mum's eyes on him.

'Of course,' he mumbled after a moment. He knew that after the way he'd behaved that morning, his mum probably wouldn't have been at all surprised if he'd said no. 'We're looking forward to it. Aren't we, Mum?'

She beamed at him. Then, 'You try stopping us. I've been excited for weeks, Denise,' she said. 'I love a good wedding.'

'I tell you what, Danny,' Denise went on, 'you should have a chat with Lily while you're both there tomorrow. You're sort of losing your dad for a while, and she's gaining a brand-new one. In a funny, roundabout, back-to-front kind of way, the pair of you have got something in common.'

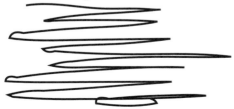

Three

After Denise and Andy's wedding service, the guests made their way to The Winville Hotel where the reception was being held.

'Glad that's over with,' muttered Lily. She climbed into the car behind Rick and his mum. 'Now we can get some food. I'm starving.'

Elaine glanced at Rick, then back towards Lily. She knew perfectly well how Lily felt about this day, but she'd already decided not to make anything of it. Not that she understood the young girl's feelings. Andy seemed like such a kind man and everyone could see how happy Denise was. But Lily was living with her for the next four and a half weeks and Elaine wanted things to go smoothly. Still, she couldn't help defending her best friend just a little.

'Your mum did look beautiful, though, didn't she?' she smiled. 'When she walked in through the door in that gorgeous dress, I thought I was going to cry. Didn't you?'

Lily shrugged.

'And did you notice what flowers she was carrying?' Elaine went on. 'Lilies! Lilies for *you*, Lily.'

'Not just for me,' Lily said. 'Lots of brides carry lilies when they get married. I've seen the pictures in Mum's magazines.'

Lily had been gazing deliberately out of the car window. Suddenly she turned to Elaine and gave her one of her sweetest smiles. 'Do you mind if we go now, Elaine? Like I said, I'm starving.'

'Yeah, me, too,' grunted Rick, hoping his mum would take the hint and leave Lily alone.

She did. It was obvious that Lily didn't want to talk about anything to do with the wedding, so Elaine gave up. She twisted round in her seat with a sideways glance at Rick, slipped on her seat belt and started the car.

The reception hotel was about half an hour's drive from Holly Hill. A smart, white-painted building, it stood at the end of a short, tarmac drive. There was a small car park off to one side. By the time Lily, Elaine and Rick had arrived, the car park was already full, so they joined the back of the short line of vehicles that had spilled out onto the drive. There was no sign of the wedding car itself. When it arrived, it would take up its specially reserved place by the main entrance door of the hotel.

'Still having their photos taken outside the church, I expect,' said Elaine as she slid out of the driver's seat. 'I'm sure they'll be here soon.'

It was warm and sunny. Other guests stood in little groups on the neatly kept lawn that sloped away from the drive. Waitresses moved between them, carrying trays of drinks and little snacks.

'People wear such fancy clothes to weddings, don't they?' Lily remarked.

'Of course they do,' smiled Elaine, adjusting her own very pink, wide-brimmed hat. 'It's a special occasion. Besides, any excuse, that's what I say. Anyway, you're looking rather smart yourself, young lady. That's such a pretty dress.'

'It's not new or anything,' Lily answered quickly. 'I didn't want a new one.'

'Well,' said Elaine, lowering her voice, 'I'll let you into a secret. Mine's not new either. And this hat? It came from a charity shop.'

'Mum,' muttered Rick, 'I'm sure Lily doesn't want to know where you do your shopping.'

'I bet she does,' Elaine replied. 'That's exactly the sort of thing girls like to know about each other.' She gave Lily a wink.

A moment later, Rick spotted Danny.

'What's he doing here?' he growled.

'Who?' asked Elaine.

'*Him.*'

Lily and Elaine followed Rick's gaze.

'Danny, you mean?' said Elaine.

Rick nodded, his eyes glinting.

'Denise probably cuts his hair. She looks after a lot of hair in Holly Hill. Now, I know he's not one of your favourite people, Rick, but you leave him alone. I don't want any trouble. Not here.'

Rick didn't answer. He didn't take his eyes off Danny either.

'No trouble, Rick,' Elaine repeated firmly. 'Promise me?'

'All right, Mum, you don't have to go on,' Rick sighed. 'I won't start anything.'

'Good boy,' she said, and turned away to continue fidgeting with her hat.

She didn't catch her son mutter under his breath, 'At least not unless he does.' But Lily did. And for the first time that day, she smiled a real smile. Rick was behaving like a Dixon – which somehow made everything feel slightly more normal.

'Let's go for a walk, shall we, Rick?' Lily suggested. 'Leave the grown-ups to their grown-uppy stuff.'

'Go on, then,' Elaine agreed. 'Not for long, though. Your mum and Andy'll be here soon and there are bound to be more photos before we eat. You know your mum's going to want you in them too, Lily.'

Lily gave just the slightest nod of her head. Then she pulled Rick away across the lawn.

'I don't want to be in their photos,' she grumbled as soon as she was sure Elaine wouldn't be able to hear. 'Why would they want me in them anyway? This whole day has got nothing to do with me.'

'It sort of has,' said Rick. 'It's *your* mum getting married.'

'Yes, but apart from that,' argued Lily. 'It's not like I want any of this to happen. That's why I said I wouldn't be a bridesmaid. I don't even want to *be* here.'

'Being a bridesmaid might have been cool, though. You might have got a present out of it.'

Lily made a face. 'I don't care. I don't even know what bridesmaids are for. They just look silly and follow the bride around carrying flowers. And come to think of it,' she continued, 'what's with all the flowers anyway? The bride and groom are supposed to be promising to love each other or something forever, aren't they? Not do gardening.'

Rick sniggered. Lily sprinted away across the grass.

Through a gate at the far end of the lawn was a children's play area. Lily pointed. 'Look at that! Your mum should have brought the twins. We could have looked after them in there.'

Rick caught her up. 'And why would we want to do that?'

'Beats hanging around with this lot.' Lily jerked her head towards the people chattering on the grass further up the slope.

At the same time, she spotted the wedding car. It had just pulled up outside the hotel. Her mum and Andy were getting out.

'And it definitely beats having my photo taken,' she muttered. 'Anyway, fancy a swing?', and she slipped through the little gate.

Lily hopped onto a blue swing seat, pushed herself backwards, then kicked her legs out. Rick followed her into the play area and stood watching as she glided backwards and forwards.

'Why don't you like him?' he asked suddenly.

'Why don't I like who?' replied Lily. Each time the swing thrust her forward, her long, black hair flew out behind her.

'Who do you think? Andy.'

Lily looked sullen. 'I never said I didn't like him. I don't like him or *not* like him. Most of the time I try not to think about him.'

'But why?' Rick persisted. 'What's he done?'

Lily didn't answer.

'Come on, Lils, he must have done something.'

'He hasn't.' Lily shook her head. 'It's just …' She thought for a moment. 'It's just what he *is*.'

'And what's that?'

Again, Lily paused. Then, 'In the way,' she murmured.

'Hello, Lily.'

At the sound of the woman's voice, both Lily and Rick turned their heads. Instantly Rick frowned. It was Danny's mum. Danny hovered awkwardly a little way behind her.

'And hello, Rick,' Danny's mum added, her tone a little less friendly. She was well aware of the Topz-Dixons run-ins. Neither Lily nor Rick said a word.

'I just wanted to say, Lily,' Danny's mum went on, 'that I know you've got Rick to stay with while your mum's away, but if you need anything and you think Danny and I can help, then we're here, too.'

Rick couldn't stop himself. 'Why would she need anything from you?' he asked gruffly.

Lily scuffed her feet on the ground to stop the swing and stared at him. She knew he didn't like Danny but she couldn't believe he could be quite so rude.

'I'm not saying you will, Lily,' answered Danny's mum quietly, deliberately not speaking to Rick. 'But if Rick's mum's busy or something like that, then we're around, too.' She smiled. 'I mean, your mum bothered to come over and do my hair for me the day before her wedding. It's the least I can do.'

Lily nodded. 'Thanks. I'm sure I'll be fine.'

She had nothing against Danny's mum – or Danny come to that – but she didn't want to annoy Rick. Not when he was being kind; not when he'd agreed to move out of his bedroom so she could sleep there. Besides, Rick was a friend. She knew Danny by sight, but that was all.

'Bit of a funny situation actually,' Danny's mum went on. 'Your mum's getting married and Danny's dad's just had to move away. Not for good but for his job.'

Danny took a step closer. 'Mum, don't,' he muttered uneasily. 'They don't want to know.'

His mum ignored him. 'It's upset you a lot, hasn't it, Danny?'

'Mum!' Danny could hardly believe she'd talk like this in front of a Dixon.

'Anyway,' she went on, 'your mum thought you and Danny might like to have a chat sometime, Lily. Thought you might have something in common. I don't know, what a lot goes on in families, eh?'

No one spoke.

'Right,' said Danny's mum into the silence. 'We'll leave you to your swinging, then.'

Danny stalked back up the slope far more quickly than his mum. At that moment he'd have been quite happy if the ground had swallowed him up. Or if he'd been carried off by a large bird. Or eaten by a small dinosaur. *Anything* so as not to have to walk away with Rick's eyes burning into his back.

Lily watched him go, too. She didn't get the chance to have another swing.

'Lily!'

Her mum was calling.

'What now?' Lily sighed.

'There you are!' Denise said. She tried to looked relaxed, but even Rick could see that her smile was fake. 'I've been looking for you, Lil. I should have known you'd be in the play park. Anyway, I need you now. We're doing photos.'

Lily raised her eyes. 'Do I have to? What do you want me in them for anyway?'

'Oh, Lily, don't be silly.' Denise forced a laugh. 'Why do you think I want you in my wedding photos? Because I love you, you daftee. Come on. Everyone's waiting.'

The wedding photographer was a tall, thin, serious looking man, with grey hair and narrow, metal-rimmed glasses. Lily couldn't help wondering how he managed to get the people in his photographs to smile when he looked as though he never smiled himself.

The photographer arranged Denise, Andy, Lily and various family members and friends, in groups and lines and huddles. He told them where to stand; to look this way, to look that way. It was impossible to tell whether he was pleased with the pictures he took. His face remained stern and serious and businesslike.

When the final photo was done, at last it was time

to eat. Lily sat next to her mum for the meal, but the moment it was finished and guests began to leave the dining room, she went looking for Rick again.

She was surprised to find him with Danny.

'I'm going to go and explore, Rick,' she said. 'Do you want to come?'

'Yeah, all right,' Rick replied. 'I was just saying to Danny, it's a shame his dad's left.'

Danny clamped his teeth together. 'He hasn't left,' he muttered. 'He's just gone away to work. He's coming back.'

'But you don't know that, do you, Danny?' Rick smirked. 'Not for sure. You only know what your parents tell you. I mean, it could be that you're never going to see him again.'

Danny shook his head. 'Idiot!' he hissed under his breath, and without even a glance at Lily, he turned and walked away.

'That was really mean, Rick,' Lily frowned. 'What did you say that for?'

Rick shrugged his shoulders. 'Why not? He's a Topz. Anyway, what's the plan now?'

Lily gazed at him for a moment. 'Well, I don't know about you,' she said, 'but I'm going to go and get lost.'

Four

Although The Winville Hotel had three floors, it wasn't a very large building so getting lost turned out to be quite hard.

Inside the front door was the main reception area with its wide, polished wooden desk and a couple of dark green sofas. From here, an arched opening led into a comfy-looking lounge scattered with deep armchairs and shiny brass lamps on side tables. One wall was full of shelves crammed with hundreds of paperback books.

The dining room was also downstairs, along with the kitchens that the guests probably never saw, and several cloakrooms.

A door marked 'private' attracted Lily's attention, but she couldn't get to it as it was behind the wooden desk at the front entrance. The receptionist there seemed very busy, but Lily was sure she'd still notice two kids trying to sneak in and have a nose around.

The two upper floors weren't very interesting either. Just corridors with numbered doors leading into bedrooms. There weren't even any people around.

Once they'd explored the third floor, Lily moaned, 'How are we supposed to get lost in here? I mean, what's the point of a hotel where you can't get lost?'

'There's always the doors,' said Rick.

'What do you mean?'

'We haven't tried any of them yet.'

'They're just bedrooms, Rick,' grumbled Lily. 'And they'll all be locked anyway.'

Rick looked at her. 'Might not be.'

'Even if we find an open one, we can't just go in.' Lily shook her head.

'Why not?'

'Because someone might be staying there. Anyway, we'd be in dead trouble if we got caught.'

Rick gave her a lopsided grin. 'Yeah, but, Lily – that's half the fun.'

Lily's eyes slid to the brass doorknob next to her, then back to Rick. 'All right, then,' she said. The corners of her mouth twitched. She could hardly believe the words were coming out of her month. 'Try that one …'

Without hesitating, Rick reached out his hand and closed his fingers around the knob.

'You absolutely sure about this?' he teased.

'*Your* idea,' Lily giggled, and her eyes sparkled. 'Nothing to do with me.'

Suddenly Rick's wrist twisted. The doorknob turned with it. He pushed.

The bedroom door remained firmly closed.

Lily burst out laughing. She wasn't sure if she was relieved or disappointed. 'I told you they'd all be locked!' she chuckled.

'What do you mean, "all"?' Rick said. 'There's more than one door along here. There are loads of them. And guess what?' he added, folding his arms. 'It's your turn to try the next one.'

Lily was still giggling as she gently tried to open the next door along. She wasn't really expecting it to budge, and it didn't. Rick wasn't put off. He moved on to the one after that, again without any luck. Then it was back to Lily's turn again.

'There's no point doing this, Rick,' Lily insisted. They'd nearly reached the other end of the corridor.

'None of these doors are going to be open. You know they're not. They lock when you close them behind you.'

Even as she spoke, the door Rick was leaning against swung back. His face broke into a huge, 'I told you so' smile. 'They're *supposed* to lock when you close them behind you,' he said smugly. 'Unless, of course, you don't shut them properly on your way out.'

Lily gaped. She looked from the door to Rick and back again.

Then, 'Close it!' she hissed. 'Close it now, before someone comes!'

Rick didn't. He pushed it open wider and stepped inside the bedroom. With a glance back at Lily, he said, 'So, are you coming in, or what?'

Lily caught her breath. She didn't know what to do. What would happen if they were caught? What would her mum say?

'I thought you wanted to get lost, Lils,' said Rick.

'I did ... I do.'

'Then, come in,' he replied, with a jerk of his head. 'Who's going to look for us in here?'

Lily looked past Rick and spotted a smart ladies' hat and cardigan on the bed. The person who was staying in this room was more than likely a wedding guest. A friend of her mum and Andy. 'No, Rick, this is someone's room and they're bound to catch us,' she whispered.

'No, they won't,' Rick insisted, 'because we'll hide.'

'Hide where?'

'I don't know. Under the bed. I tell you what, Lily, if we're going to be living together for a month, you're going to have to learn to trust me.'

Lily blinked at him. She took one look over her shoulder.

The corridor was empty. There was no one to see them.

Just do it, she thought to herself.

In another moment, she'd stepped inside.

Danny was by himself. His heels rested on the ground as he rocked backwards and forwards on a swing in the play area at the hotel. His eyes stung. He wanted to cry but he couldn't let himself. Not here at someone's wedding celebration. Not here where Rick, the Dixon, might see him.

Danny wasn't sure where his mum was. Somewhere in amongst the crowd of guests scattered about the hotel. She seemed to be telling almost everyone she talked to that his dad had just gone to Spain to work.

'Why do you want people to know about Dad?' he'd asked at the end of the meal.

'I don't especially,' his mum had replied. 'It just helps to talk about it, I suppose.'

It hadn't helped Danny. The last person in the world he wanted to know anything about him was a Dixon. His mum had told Lily his dad had gone away in front of Rick. Now Rick could tease him about it, and he hadn't wasted any time in doing exactly that.

I don't want to be here.

Danny mouthed his prayer silently. The only ears he wanted to hear him were God's.

I don't want to be here, God. I don't know why we had to come to this stupid wedding. I don't know why

Dad couldn't have gone away tomorrow instead of yesterday. Then he could have come instead of me. I'm only here to keep Mum company and now I don't even know where she is. I'm not looking for her. I don't want to see anybody. I just want to go home.

I wonder how many days Dixons have wrecked for Topz since we've all been living in Holly Hill? Must be loads and loads. As if things aren't bad enough now Dad's not around any more, Rick knows he's gone. And Rick has to be here, too, doesn't he? Sticking his nose in. Saying horrible stuff. Dad's coming back to visit, I know he is. Lots of times. And as soon as he finds another job here he won't have to work in Spain any more. It's work, that's all it is. That's the only reason he's gone away. But Rick has to go and make it sound like Mum and Dad are splitting up or something. Why does he have to do that, God? Why does he have to be so nasty? He didn't have to say anything at all. Except that he's a Dixon, isn't he, and that's what Dixons do. They make everything worse.

Mum wants me to make friends with Lily. She reckons we'll be able to 'understand each other's feelings' or something. She thinks we can help each other. But help each other how exactly? Mum says Lily never knew her dad. So how can she possibly understand what it feels like when your dad has to go away? A long way away. And I've never had a stepdad so how am I supposed to know what that's like? We can't help each other at all, God. I don't know what Mum's talking about. Anyway I'll never make friends with Lily because she's staying with Rick. Of everyone she could possibly have gone to stay with, her mum had to pick a Dixon!

So that's it. I don't care what Mum wants. I'm not having anything to do with Lily. She won't want to know me, either. Not if she's mates with Rick. He's probably told her to hate me. Well, do You know what, God, right now I hate Rick. I know that You say we should never hate anyone, but I do. I don't see why I should be nice to him.

I HATE HIM.

'Danny? What are you doing out here all on your own?' Danny's mum stood at the gate to the play area. 'I've been looking for you. Are you all right?'

Danny shook his head. 'Not really. I was hoping we could go home soon.'

'What's the matter?' his mum asked. 'Aren't you enjoying yourself?'

'Rick from Dixons is here,' he replied sulkily. 'How could I be enjoying myself?'

'I know, but Lily's here, too. I thought you might have been able to have a little chat with her by now. Not that anyone seems to know where she is at the moment,' she added. 'You haven't seen her, have you, Danny? Denise says she and Andy have to leave for the airport soon and she can't find her anywhere.'

'Haven't a clue,' Danny muttered. 'But I'll bet if she can find Rick, she'll find Lily.'

Danny's mum shook her head and sighed. 'I know. I do hope Denise knows what she's doing leaving her with that boy. Oh, come and help find her, will you, Danny? Denise and Andy can't miss their flight.'

Danny made a face. 'Mum, do I have to?' he groaned.

'Just come and help, Danny,' his mum insisted.

'As soon as we've found her, Denise and Andy can leave. Then we can go home.'

Five

The first time Lily's phone rang, it startled her so much, she squealed and collapsed into fits of giggles. It was now ringing in her pocket for the sixth time and it wasn't funny any more. Not at all.

Lily and Rick were huddled together on the floor in the hotel bedroom. When they'd first stepped inside, they'd crawled underneath the bed to hide. But before long, it had got so hot and stuffy in the tiny space they were jammed into that they'd had to drag themselves out again. At least they could stay on the far side of the bed from the door. If they kept low to the floor and anyone came in they shouldn't be spotted immediately. They might just have time to wriggle back underneath the bed before anyone realised they were there.

'Why don't you just answer it?' Rick asked. He was beginning to get fed up. Hiding in the room had been fun until Lily's phone started to go off.

'I told you. It's Mum,' she answered moodily. 'They've probably got to go soon and she wants to say goodbye.'

'Go and say goodbye, then.'

The phone stopped ringing. 'I don't want to,' Lily murmured. 'I don't want to see her.' After a moment, there was a bleep. Lily's mum had left yet another message.

'Just listen to her messages, then,' Rick said. 'In fact, if you really don't want to see her, you could ring and leave *her* a message saying goodbye.'

It was meant as a joke. But suddenly Lily's eyes were full of tears.

'I don't want to leave her a message!' she blurted out.

'I don't want her to go! If she can't find me to say goodbye, then she *can't* go, can she?'

Rick shifted on the floor uncomfortably. He didn't know what to say. He wasn't used to dealing with tears; apart from his little sisters' and they never cried about anything important. Just over whose turn it was to watch TV, or a squabble about a toy, or because they didn't want to go to bed. Lily was really upset. Rick didn't know what to do. Part of him wanted to leave her to it.

'Why don't you want her to go?' he mumbled at last.

Lily sniffed and brushed away her tears. 'Why do you think? Would you be happy if your mum was about to fly off to New Zealand and leave you here on your own?'

'You're *not* on your own. You're with us.'

Lily sighed. 'You know what I mean.'

'But you could have gone,' Rick answered. 'They did ask you.'

'No, I couldn't!' Lily turned her tear-streaked face towards him. 'You don't get it. Nobody gets it! They only asked because they felt they had to. They don't really want me to go.'

Rick frowned. 'That's stupid.'

'No, it's not. When your mum said I could stay with you, Mum jumped at it, didn't she? It made it so easy for her.'

'You don't know what you're talking about,' Rick muttered.

'Yeah, well, neither do you.'

There was silence.

'You're going to have to go and find her,' Rick said at last. 'We can't stay in here forever, can we?'

Hardly were the words out of his mouth when the

bedroom door swung open and a woman walked in.

So much for the plan to slip back underneath the bed out of sight. The two of them had been so deep in conversation they'd almost forgotten they weren't supposed to be there. Shocked that someone had actually come in, they froze.

It's just possible that the lady whose room they were in might not have spotted them. She headed straight to the mirror in the bathroom to fiddle with her hair.

But then Lily's phone rang again – and frightened all three of them half to death.

'What in the world do you think you're doing?' the woman shrieked. 'Ooh, you nearly gave me a heart attack!'

'I'm sorry.'

Lily was sure she'd said the words at least a hundred times, but her mum was still furious.

'You went and hid in someone's room,' she kept saying, over and over again. 'Someone's room where you had no right to be. You know, sometimes, Lily, you astonish me, you really do. And not in a good way!'

'But we weren't doing anything wrong. We were just *in* there.'

'Exactly! You were in there when you shouldn't have been!'

Elaine was furious, too. She couldn't believe Rick had let her down so badly.

'I was just trying to cheer Lily up,' he said.

'What, by getting her into trouble?' Elaine snapped.

Rick raised his eyes. 'It was meant to be a laugh.'

'Was it really?' muttered Elaine. 'Well, guess what, Rick? The only one who's finding any of this even the tiniest bit funny is you! Denise doesn't know if she wants to leave Lily with us now! And that's all your fault!'

Denise, Andy and Lily stood outside near the hotel main entrance.

'How can I go away and leave you, Lily, if you're going to be getting up to stuff like this?' Denise frowned. 'One afternoon. *One* afternoon when I'm not keeping an eye on you, and look what's happened. I can't spend the next month worried sick about you, I just can't.'

Andy was the only one to stay calm. 'Lily's a good girl, Denise,' he said gently. 'You know she is. And you didn't touch anything in the room, did you, Lily? You didn't break anything or steal anything. All right, so you shouldn't have gone in there. But, honestly, Denise, it's not worth getting this upset about. It's happened and

Lily's said she's sorry. Lots of times. Now, if we don't get ready to leave, we're going to miss our plane.'

It was weird, Lily thought, how Andy was the only one *not* treating what she and Rick had done like the crime of the century. He didn't appear cross at all. If anything, he seemed more amused that everyone else was getting so upset.

But then, Andy wouldn't want to miss his holiday in New Zealand, would he? So he'd have to do what he could to smooth things over to make sure Denise still went with him. That's what Lily supposed as she listened to the two of them; the one voice trembling with stress and worry; the other, calm and reasonable.

Most of the wedding guests didn't know what had happened as they gathered at the hotel main entrance to wave the bride and groom goodbye. Lily's Auntie Mandy was driving them back to Holly Hill so that they could pick up the bags they'd packed ready for their trip. Then she would take them on to the airport. With everyone clustered together outside the front door, Denise gave Lily a final hug.

As she clasped her in her arms, she whispered into her daughter's ear, 'I love you, Lil. Please, *please* be good for me. I'll text you loads. I'll phone as well, and I'll be back before you know it. And I do love you. I promise you, I do love you.'

She pulled away, her cheeks all wet with tears. Lily's flowed, too. She couldn't speak. The only way to keep her sobs under control was to press her lips tightly together so that her teeth dug into them.

Elaine stood next to her as the car pulled away. She wanted to reach for Lily's hand; to give it a squeeze to let her know that everything would be all right.

But she didn't. Just then, she didn't think Lily would want anyone to comfort her.

She was right. All Lily wanted was her mum.

And her mum had gone.

With Auntie Mandy's car out of sight, the wedding guests started to drift off. Some went back into the hotel, some wandered off across the lawn, a few headed for their cars.

'What do you want to do, Lily, darling?' Elaine asked kindly. Rick hovered uncomfortably beside her. 'Do you want to stay for a bit longer or do you want to go home? I've got to be back before too long to pick up the twins but we don't have to leave right away if you don't want to.'

Lily swallowed hard. It was still a struggle to speak. She wanted to be on her own. Not just for now, but forever. But she could hardly say that to Elaine.

'Can I just go for a walk round the hotel?' she gulped at last. She didn't look at Rick as she added, 'By myself?'

Elaine hesitated. Lily knew what she was thinking. 'I won't do anything wrong, Elaine,' she said quietly. 'I won't go where I'm not supposed to. Promise.'

'Go on, then,' Elaine agreed. 'You sure you don't want Rick to go with you?'

Lily shook her head. 'No. Sorry, Rick, I just want to be on my own for a bit.'

'Fine by me,' Rick shrugged. He was relieved. He wouldn't have known what to say anyway.

'Half an hour, then, Lily,' said Elaine. 'You be back here in half an hour. Have you got a watch?'

'I've got my phone.'

'Half an hour, then.'

Lily didn't go back to the play park. There were other

43

children around and she was sure they'd have found it by now. Instead she made her way around the other side of the hotel, away from the lawn. It was quieter here. None of the other guests had come this way. But there were no signs saying 'private' so she thought it must be all right.

She followed the gravel path a little way, then clambered up a grassy bank. A short distance away was a curved line of trees. Lily spotted the wooden bench standing underneath them a second before she noticed the boy sprawled on the grass with his back against it. As soon as he saw Lily, he scrambled to his feet.

'All right?' Danny asked hesitantly.

Lily really wasn't interested in talking to anyone. But oddly, she had something she wanted to say to Danny. Now was as good a time as any.

She took a few steps closer, folded her arms and shook her head. 'Not really. I don't know. Are you supposed to enjoy it when your mum gets married?'

Danny had spoken to Lily because he felt he ought to. He wasn't expecting her to answer. He hoped the surprise didn't show on his face.

'I couldn't say. Sorry,' he replied. 'I wasn't around when my mum got married.'

Lily nodded. 'I just wanted to say sorry for what Rick said earlier. About your dad not coming back. I don't know what made him do that. It was horrible.'

This time, Danny was lost for words. He stood still, blinking at her.

'I mean it, I'm really sorry,' Lily went on. 'I like Rick but I know he can be nasty sometimes. I suppose it's because his dad left, but he shouldn't have picked on you about yours.' She paused. 'I was thinking, though.

All three of us ... we're a bit the same. Did you know that?'

Danny frowned. A bit the same? What was she talking about?

'I don't understand what you mean,' he said.

'It's easy,' Lily replied. There was a matter-of-factness in her voice. 'Your dad's left you for a while. My mum's left me. And Rick – well, his dad's gone completely. Moved away and never coming back.' She stopped and narrowed her eyes. 'Are you getting it now?'

For another moment, Danny didn't get it at all. Then suddenly, what Lily had tried to say clicked into place inside his head.

Slowly, he nodded. 'The same thing's happened to us in different ways,' he said quietly. 'But none of us wanted it to.'

Lily gave him a sad smile. 'Yeah. And none of us can do anything about it either.'

Six

Danny was wide awake. There were too many thoughts rattling around in his head to let him sleep.

There was also rain clattering loudly against his bedroom window. The late spring skies had stayed clear for Denise and Andy's wedding, but later that evening, it had started to drizzle. Now the rain was pouring down. A strong wind kept catching it in gusts and seemed to be hurling it against whatever made the most noise.

For about the tenth time, Danny rolled over and picked up his clock. He pressed the button to turn on the light that illuminated the face.

Two o'clock in the morning.

How could it only be two o'clock in the morning? He felt as though he'd been lying in bed forever.

He sat up and clicked on the lamp beside his bed. Light flooded his room and hurt his eyes. Screwing them up, he reached for his Bible. The postcard still marked the page in the Book of Romans.

Danny read the verse out loud; the same verse he somehow couldn't stop reading to himself over and over again: *'We know that in all things God works for good with those who love him ...'*

I do trust You, God.

Danny whispered the words and they made him smile. He was fairly sure that right then and there, sitting up in bed in the middle of the night listening to the rain – he trusted God completely.

I was wrong, wasn't I? About everything to do with Lily. I thought I could never be her friend. I thought we couldn't help each other. I thought she'd hate me because she's friends with Rick.

But we can help each other, can't we? We sort of understand each other because we're going through the same kind of thing. And Lily doesn't hate me at all. I really think she wants to be my friend. Not sure how that's going to work while she's staying with Rick. But there's afterwards, isn't there, God? After her mum gets back. Maybe she'll still want to be friends then. I guess what's weird is that, if Dad hadn't gone away then Lily and I might never have talked to each other properly. So that's one good thing that's happened with Dad going to Spain.

Dad rang when I got home. He sounds all right but he says he's missing us. Mum and me. He says he's glad he feels sad, though. He said, 'It reminds me how lucky I am to have a family I love so much that it hurts to be away from them.' Something like that anyway. I said, 'So you'll be coming home soon, then?' and he said, 'Yeah!'

I hope it is soon, God. Please look after him in Spain. Please look after us in Holly Hill – Mum, me. Lily. Oh yes, and I'm sorry I said I hated Rick, God. I don't hate him. I don't think I'll ever understand him, but I don't hate him. Not really.

One more thing. Could You, please, help me get to sleep now?

Lily sat at the top of the slide in the park. It was wet from the night's rain but she didn't care.

Rick watched her as she peered down at her phone, reading a text. 'Is it your mum?' he asked.

Lily shook her head. 'Auntie Mandy. Just saying let her know if I need anything. Shall I text back and say, "Yes, lots of chocolate"? It wouldn't have been Mum anyway. They won't be in New Zealand yet. It takes ages to get there, Andy said.'

'Does it?' Rick replied.

'Of course it does,' said Lily. 'It's the other side of the world at least. I reckon it's a bit like time travelling.'

Rick raised his eyebrows at her. 'How do you work that out?'

'New Zealand is loads of hours ahead of us, isn't it? It's morning here, but over there it must be nearly night-time by now. So all the people in New Zealand have had today already.' Lily shrugged. 'Which basically means that when Mum gets there, she'll have gone forward in time.'

'Right.' Rick wasn't going to pretend he understood what Lily was talking about. A lot of the things she came out with he found confusing.

He didn't expect it at all when she suddenly asked, 'Why don't you Dixons like the Topz Gang?'

'What?'

'You heard. Come on, tell me. I want to know.'

Rick stared at her for a minute. Then, 'You can be really annoying, do you know that?' he growled.

Lily slipped her phone into her pocket and pushed off

down the slide. At the bottom she stood and tilted her head to one side as she looked at him.

'Well, do you know what I think?' she said. 'I don't think you even know.'

Rick didn't get the chance to answer. A football shot through the air towards him, almost skimming the top of his head. He whirled around to see the other two Dixons, Clyde and Kevin, racing towards him with broad grins on their faces.

'You missed!' Rick yelled.

'Only 'cos you moved!' Clyde shouted back.

'I did not move!' Rick retorted.

'You must have,' argued Clyde. ''Cos I had you dead on.'

Kevin glanced at Lily. 'All right?' he grunted.

Although Lily was in the Dixons Gang's class at Southlands, it was just Rick who sometimes saw her outside of school, and that was only because their mums were friends. But that would change for the next month while she was staying with him. She'd be around much more. Clyde and Kevin weren't sure they were happy about it.

'So is your mum married now, Lily?' Clyde asked bluntly.

Lily looked at him. 'Yup,' she said after a moment, equally bluntly. 'So are you ever going to learn to kick a football straight, Clyde?'

Clyde frowned, but Rick answered for him. 'Not a chance,' he smirked. Then, 'Bin. Over there,' he added, drawing back his right foot and punching the ball across the grass where it smacked into a concrete litterbin.

'Woohoo!' he howled, throwing his fists triumphantly into the air. 'And you know you will never be as good as me, Clyde!'

Lily couldn't help smiling at the scowl on Clyde's face.

He stuck his hands into his pockets and stalked off after the ball.

'Are you playing, Rick?' asked Kevin.

Rick glanced at Lily. 'Yeah, probably. In a bit.'

He and Lily watched Kevin as he chased after Clyde, overtaking him and swiping the ball from under his nose.

'You can go and play now if you want,' said Lily. 'You don't have to stay with me all the time.'

'I know,' replied Rick. But he didn't move.

Lily eyed him for a moment. 'Are Kevin and Clyde your best mates?' she asked.

Rick nodded. 'Yeah, I suppose they are.'

'Do you trust them?'

Rick raised his eyes. 'Why do you ask so many questions?' he answered.

'It's how you find out about people. Anyway, yesterday you said I'd have to learn to trust you. I was wondering who *you* trust.'

'So you're just nosey, then,' Rick chuckled.

'And you're a pain because you don't like answering questions.'

Rick held his hands up in defeat and sighed. 'All right, all right. I trust them. I mean it's not something I ever really think about but, yeah. They're my mates so I trust them. Satisfied now?'

'Nearly,' Lily smiled. 'What about me? Do you trust me?'

Rick was starting to feel exasperated. There seemed to be no stopping this girl. 'I dunno, do I?' he said. 'I don't know you like I know them. But … I guess I trust you. Sort of. Why do you want to know anyway?'

'Because,' Lily replied, 'if I trust *you*, you should trust *me*. Like you said, especially if we've got to live together for a month. I think we ought to test it out.'

Rick shook his head. Lily was making his head spin. He frowned at her. 'What are you getting at now?'

'Let's play a trust game,' she said.

'You're so weird,' was all Rick replied.

'No, I'm not. Look, I followed you into that hotel bedroom, didn't I?'

'Yeah,' Rick muttered. 'Maybe you shouldn't have.'

'I still did it. Because you wanted me to trust you. So, how about you do something for me? How about … you go and have a slide – with your eyes closed?'

'*What?*'

'It's easy. Close your eyes, climb up the steps and slide down. With your eyes closed.'

'Oh, that sounds like a *really* good idea,' Rick scoffed. 'It's quite high when you get up to the top. You sort of *need* to have your eyes open.'

Lily smiled. 'No, you don't. You're missing the point. The minute you close your eyes, I'll tell you where to put your feet. I'll tell you when you've reached the top step. I'll tell you when to sit down. You won't fall, I won't let you. But you've got to keep your eyes closed *the whole* time. Otherwise it won't work. You won't be trusting me.'

Rick would have laughed if he thought Lily was joking. But he knew she wasn't.

'I can't, can I?' He nodded his head towards Kevin and Clyde who were still kicking the football around in the distance. 'They'll think I'm as mad as you.'

Lily folded her arms. 'Who cares?'

This wasn't a dare. If it was, Rick would have done it almost without thinking about it. But it wasn't. It was one of crazy Lily's crazy ideas. There was a part of Rick that was growing to quite like that craziness.

'I can't make you out,' he said. 'You're a right puzzle, do you know that?'

Lily's eyes narrowed. 'Why do you say that?'

' Because you are … Ergh … All right, let's do it. But can we be quick before they see?'

'As quick as you like,' Lily grinned. 'As quick as you can trust me.'

A short distance from the bottom of the slide's metal steps, Lily said, 'Close your eyes, Rick.'

He glanced again towards Clyde and Kevin. They weren't looking his way. They were too interested in their game.

So Rick closed his eyes.

'Hold out your arms,' instructed Lily. Rick did as he was told. 'Now, walk forward very slowly until you reach the railings.'

Rick shuffled forward until his hands found the railings that ran up either side of the steps. His fingers closed around them.

'Can you feel the first step?' Lily asked.

Rick moved one foot around until he could. He stood on the step with both feet.

'Keep going like that. One step at a time.'

So far this was easy. Nothing to it. But the higher up Rick clambered, the more he wanted to open his eyes. Just to check where he was. He didn't like the feeling of not knowing how far up he'd climbed.

He stopped. 'Where am I, Lily? How far am I from the top?'

'I'm right behind you,' Lily answered. As soon as he'd started to climb, she'd followed. 'I'm two steps away. You're not going to fall.'

'But am I nearly there?'

'I'm not telling you. When you're at the top, I'll let you know, I promise. Don't open your eyes.'

'I don't know why I'm doing this,' Rick muttered as he started again, feeling his way up the steps. He didn't open his eyes, though. Lily was still behind him and if he did, he felt sure she'd know.

Finally, he heard her say, 'Next one's the top one.'

Lily waited until both Rick's feet were planted firmly on the last step.

'Now,' she said softly, 'all you've got to do is sit down – and slide.'

It felt strange. Rick knew exactly where he was – how high up he was. He'd been up there a thousand times. But without being able to see, it was suddenly frightening.

Still grasping tightly onto the railings, Rick lowered himself carefully into a sitting position.

'Don't open your eyes,' Lily said again. 'Not till you reach the bottom.'

Rick let go with his hands and pushed off. In the darkness behind his closed eyes, he felt as though he was falling … falling into a pit of blackness … faster and faster …

Until his body slowed and stopped and he was back on the ground.

He opened his eyes, gulped in a breath and twisted round.

Lily stood at the top of the slide gazing down at him.

'You see? Told you I wouldn't let you fall,' she smiled. 'Now you know you can trust me.'

Seven

Hi Danny.

Danny happened to be at the computer when the email from his dad clicked in.

How was school? I hope it's keeping you busy. I've been very busy here today. I've had a guided tour round the factory and met most of the people I'm going to be working with. I think I know where everything is now, but it's all going to take a bit of getting used to. Especially as my Spanish isn't up to much!

Very excited to find that the canteen does jolly good chips, though. Lovely and crispy. You'd like them.

Thanks for going to the wedding with Mum. From what you said on the phone, it sounds as if you quite enjoyed it in the end. Have you seen your friend, Lily, again?

I miss you, Danny. You and your mum. I know this is hard but we'll all get through it. I'll keep looking for jobs at home and the minute something comes up, I'll be back. Then you'll probably be telling me I'm in the way!

Must stop for now. I'm being taken on a tour of the town this evening. Not that that'll help me find my way round. You know what my sense of direction's like.

Take care, Danny, and speak to you soon.

Lots of love

Dad x

Danny read through the email twice. The second time, he clicked 'Reply'.

Hi Dad.

School's OK, thanks. Well, except for Paul having to go to hospital at lunchtime. Benny had this idea of doing a leapfrog race. (I won't explain. It's complicated.)

Anyway, it was all fine until Paul was leapfrogging over John. He landed funny and sprained his ankle. It swelled up really quickly! You should have seen it! It wasn't Benny's fault but he felt SO bad because the race was his idea. Paul was funny, though. When we saw him later, he said, 'Don't worry about it, Benny. It could have been worse. I could have broken my glasses, too. Then I wouldn't have been able to see as well as not being able to walk!'

I won't tell Mum about the chips. I think she thought the weather would be so hot where you are you'd only be eating salads. She said she was pleased to think you'd be eating healthy food. Maybe you had salad with your chips.

Yes, I saw Lily today after school. I was in the corner shop and she came in to buy sweets. I didn't really talk to her much because she was with Rick. She asked if I was all right, and if you'd rung, so I told her you had. But when I asked if she'd spoken to her mum, she said no. She said her mum had rung but she didn't want to talk to her. Not until she'd been away for a bit longer. She said she'd only get upset if she heard her mum's voice. I think she's texted her a few times, though. Rick didn't say a word. He just stood there staring at me the whole time. Then he suddenly told Lily they needed to hurry up, so we said bye and that was it really.

Lily's not exactly my friend, Dad. I've hardly spoken to her. She just seems nice. I wish she didn't have to stay with Rick. I mean I suppose her mum wouldn't have left her with Rick's family if she didn't think it would be all right, but Rick's already landed her in trouble once by taking her into that room in the hotel. Remember I told you about that when you rang? I hope he doesn't try to get her to do anything else she shouldn't. Like I say, I think she's nice and she doesn't deserve to end up being yelled at because of a Dixon. I hope she'll be all right. I mean, she's not all right because her mum's gone away. And it must be weird thinking that when her mum gets back everything will be different because she'll have a stepdad. At least when you get back, everything'll be the same.

Anyway, better go. We've started a new project about spiders and I wanted to find some good pictures on the internet.

Miss you, Dad. Wish you were coming home at the weekend.

Don't eat too many chips. If you do, I might have to tell Mum.

Bye.

Love

Danny xx

Lily sat next to Rick at the top of one of the skateboard ramps in the park. Rick had a scowl on his face. The scowl deepened as he shook his head when Lily offered him one of the sweets she'd just bought at the corner shop.

Lily peered at him hard. 'Are you in a bad mood with me?' she demanded.

'What? No!' Rick muttered.

Lily nodded. 'You are, aren't you? I knew it. Is it because I just spoke to Danny?'

Rick shrugged his shoulders moodily. 'Nothing to do with me who you talk to.'

'Well, you got that right,' Lily said. 'No, it's not. Anyway, you still haven't told me why you don't like Danny. Why do Dixons hate Topz so much?'

'They're just a bunch of goody-goodies, all right? They wind us up. They're always making out like they're so perfect. Always going on about God.'

'God?' Lily looked surprised. 'Are they?' Then she smiled and elbowed Rick in the ribs. 'It's not a very good reason to hate someone, though, is it?'

Rick didn't answer.

'Anyway, I like Danny,' Lily went on. 'He seems OK to me.'

'Well, don't expect *me* to like him, that's all,' Rick growled.

'I won't. And don't expect *me* not to talk to him, that's all,' she mimicked.

For a second Rick looked cross. But then, grudgingly, he smiled. Lily held out her bag of sweets to him again. This time he took one. They both sat chewing.

'What time do we have to be home?' Lily asked.

'Doesn't matter. Why?'

'Have we got maybe a couple of hours?'

'Why?' he said again.

'I was just wondering,' Lily replied, 'whether you'd like a bit of an adventure?'

Rick's eyes narrowed suspiciously. 'What do you mean? What sort of an adventure?'

'Say yes and I'll tell you.'

Rick didn't answer. He was remembering going down the slide with his eyes closed.

'Oh, come on, Rick,' Lily said. 'I thought you trusted me.'

Rick raised his eyes. 'All right, yes. Now tell me.'

Lily beamed at him. 'Let's get the bus to where I used to live. I can show you my old house.'

'And that's what you call an adventure, is it?' Rick didn't look impressed.

'Yeah. I've not been back there in ages. Mum never wants to go.'

'So why do you want to go back there now?'

Lily shook her head impatiently. 'Does there have to be a reason for everything? Look it's only about half an hour away. Maybe a bit more. And I know where the bus goes from and I've got money. Please, Rick.'

Rick pulled his phone out of his pocket.

'What are you doing?' Lily asked.

'Texting Mum. She'll be mad if I don't tell her what we're doing. Apparently I'm supposed to be looking after you or something.'

'I don't need looking after. Rick, *please* don't say where we're going.'

Rick sighed. No wonder he liked hanging around with Kevin and Clyde. It was never this complicated doing stuff with Dixons. 'Why not?'

'Because if anyone knows, it won't be an adventure, will it?'

Rick fiddled with his phone. Then he began to punch in a message with his thumb.

'Rick!' Lily glared at him.

'Well, I've got to say something, haven't I?' Rick jabbed 'send' then looked into Lily's annoyed face. 'Don't look so worried,' he muttered. 'I just told her we're staying out for a bit and we'll be back later.'

Lily stood up and shuffled down the skateboard ramp. When she looked back at Rick, he was still sitting at the top.

She stuffed the bag of sweets into the rucksack on her shoulder. Then she put her hands on her hips. 'Well, come on then,' she said. 'Let's go.'

They didn't have to wait long for a bus. Fursley, the village where Lily used to live, was on one of the main routes so there were three buses an hour from Holly Hill. Getting back wouldn't be a problem either. Rick's mum had texted to see what time they'd be home.

'Tell her seven o'clock,' said Lily. 'We'll easily be back by then.'

Forty minutes or so later, the bus had turned off the main road and was pulling up at the stop outside Fursley post office.

Lily jumped off excitedly. Rick followed, hands in his pockets, still not sure why he seemed to have let himself get pushed into this.

'So, this is Fursley,' Lily announced. 'I can't believe you've never been here before.'

'Well, why would I?' Rick glanced around. 'It's not exactly the centre of the universe, is it?'

Fursley had once been a tiny village, but over the years it had gradually sprawled out from its edges as more and more houses had been built. It was still much smaller than Holly Hill but it didn't seem to be any quieter. The road running through the centre was very busy. Rick and Lily had to keep well in on the pavement.

Lily walked quickly and Rick found himself hurrying to keep up.

'Can we slow down a bit?' he asked.

'Nope,' Lily answered, without turning round. 'We haven't got long if we've got to be back by seven. I just want to get there.'

'How far is it?'

'Just round the corner.'

In fact, Lily's old house was round several corners and along two left turns. It was the last in a line of five red brick, terraced cottages down a little road called Bailey Place. As soon as she set eyes on them, Lily stopped dead.

What had happened here?

This had been her home. Where she and her mum had been happy. They'd moved away two years ago and now it didn't look as though anyone lived in Bailey Place at all. The cottages – all five of them – appeared deserted. Big boards had been nailed across the windows and doors, and the front gardens were wild with weeds and litter. Weeds were even pushing their way through the tarmac where the garden walls met the pavement. There were several large 'keep out' signs, too, warning people away.

Rick's eyes scanned the houses then darted towards Lily.

'I'm guessing it wasn't like this when you lived here,' he said slowly.

Lily didn't answer. She just shook her head vaguely and walked towards the end of the terrace, stopping outside her old front gate.

'Is this it, then?' wondered Rick. 'Was this your house?'

'I don't understand,' Lily murmured. 'This was our home. I was born here. Upstairs in that bedroom.' She pointed to a boarded up opening on the first floor. 'Right there. Why would someone do this?'

'Dunno,' Rick shrugged. 'Must be a good reason, though.'

There was the sound of footsteps. Lily spun round. A lady was walking past on the other side of road.

Lily didn't hesitate. 'Excuse me!' she called. 'Do you know what's happened to these houses?'

The lady looked slightly surprised but she still stopped for a moment to answer.

'They're going to be knocked down, dear.'

Lily's face fell even further. 'Knocked down? Why? What's wrong with them?'

The lady smiled. 'There's nothing wrong with the houses, dear. It's because of the new road. They're building a bypass to keep more of the traffic out of the centre of the village. It's going to go right through the middle of them.'

'Well, when?' Lily persisted. 'When are they building it?

At that the lady gave a snort of laughter. 'Your guess is as good as mine, dearie,' she said. 'You know what these councils are like. I think the houses were bought up a good two years ago, but nothing's happened so far.'

The lady continued walking and disappeared through the railings at the end where the road turned into a footpath.

Lily looked back at the house. 'That's when we moved,' she murmured. 'Two years ago.'

'So?' asked Rick.

'So,' replied Lily quietly, 'Mum must have known about it. That's why she never wants to come back here. She didn't want me to find out.'

There was a pause, then suddenly Lily was heading for her old front gate.

'Wait a minute, Lils, where are you going now?' Rick demanded.

'I'm going to see if I can get in round the back.'

Rick looked at her, flabbergasted. 'Get *in*? Are you nuts?'

Lily didn't stop. 'No. It's my house, I'm allowed.'

'It's *not* your house. Not any more. You can't go in there.'

'Well, I'm going to try.' Lily turned briefly and looked at him. 'Are you coming with me?'

'Lily, you don't even know if it's safe.'

'Of course it's safe. It's my old house.'

Rick didn't move. He stood staring at her. Dixons had done some crazy things in the past, but he wasn't at all sure he liked the sound of this.

Suddenly, 'Just forget it,' Lily muttered. 'I'll go in without you.'

And then she was gone. Down the front path, round the side of the house and out of sight.

Eight

'Wait!' Rick hissed.

By the time he'd caught up with her, Lily had dropped her rucksack and was already wrenching at the boarding at one of the downstairs windows. She'd managed to loosen one corner, but she couldn't pull the board out far enough to allow her to get at the window underneath.

'Let me try,' muttered Rick.

Lily stood back and Rick began to yank at it. Gradually, he worked the nails loose until the board was left hanging by one corner.

The window glass was broken. Rick held the board to one side while Lily pushed what was left of it inside the building with a stick. The pieces fell into the kitchen sink that stood just underneath. There were a few jagged edges left, but the opening was big enough for them to get through without catching themselves.

Placing her hands flat on the windowsill, Lily pushed down, then sprang up to sit on it. From there, she was able to swing her legs carefully round until her feet were in the sink. She bent her head, grasped the sink edge and pulled herself the rest of the way through the opening. Moments later, she was standing on the kitchen floor, watching Rick go through the same process.

Lily smiled at him. 'I knew you wanted to see really.'

'Yeah, well, we should be quick,' Rick grunted.

Lily cast her eyes around the kitchen. Her mum had taken the red-painted table and chairs with them when they moved. Now the fitted cupboards were gone, too; ripped away from the walls leaving torn wallpaper and bare plaster where they'd once stood. All that was left in there was the sink. The room looked so different. So huge in its emptiness. She tried to picture how it had been before; as the place where she'd played and enjoyed meals and stood on a chair at the sink to help her mum with the washing up. Lily could see it all in her mind. But somehow she couldn't seem to make any of it fit into this bare, derelict-looking space.

'This *used* to be our kitchen,' she said sadly. 'Let's go and have a look at what *used* to be our lounge.'

With the windows boarded up, there was very little daylight getting into the house. There were no bulbs in the light fittings either. Even if there had been, the electricity to the cottage had long ago been cut off.

The greatest amount of light came from the kitchen window, where the two of them had opened it up. It trickled through into the hall, but it was still very dim the further inside they moved. Only a little late afternoon sunshine managed to filter its way in around the edges of the window boards.

The lounge was easier to imagine as Lily remembered it. The furniture had obviously gone, but everything else was the same: the open fireplace, the mantelshelf above it and the cupboard built into the wall in one corner.

Her eyes growing used to the murky light, Lily reached out her hand and smoothed it over the dingy-looking wallpaper.

'It's the same,' she murmured. 'I remember the walls looking like this. A bit cleaner maybe.'

Rick glanced at his phone. 'It's nearly six o'clock, Lily. We should go or we'll be late back.'

'I thought you Dixons weren't bothered about being late home.' Lily still gazed at the wallpaper.

'If I was *with* Dixons I wouldn't be,' Rick retorted. 'But I'm with you, and Mum doesn't even know where you are.'

'Let's go upstairs.' It was as if Lily hadn't heard him.

'Lily!' Rick snapped.

'We'll be quick, I promise,' she answered. 'It's not long back to the bus stop from here. I just want to see my room.'

She headed for the stairs.

'Lily, it's *not* your room any more. We don't even know if it's safe up there.'

'Of course it's safe.' In a moment, she'd made her way up to the landing. Her black school shoes clunked across the bare floorboards. It was even darker up here.

The bathroom was straight ahead of her. As with the kitchen, Lily could just about see that everything had been torn out. In the scraps of light at the edges of the windows, it looked a mess of dust and rubble and broken tiles.

Lily's bedroom stood next to it. She could make out the half-open door. One part of her was afraid to go in. What would she find?

A harsh brightness suddenly burst through the darkness. It startled her, but only for a moment. Rick was standing behind her holding up his phone. It sent out a bluish glare.

'Good idea,' said Lily. She reached into her pocket for her own phone, pressed a key and it lit up, too. 'We'll have to bring torches next time.'

'Next time?' Rick frowned. 'What do you mean "next time"? I'm not doing this again.'

Once more Lily seemed not to hear him. With her phone in one hand, throwing out its garish light, she

stepped forward and pushed on her old bedroom door.
The hinges squeaked uncomfortably as it swung back.
Lily wondered when it had last been opened.

Using the light from their phones, they gazed around the empty room. Again, the wallpaper was just as Lily remembered – a whitish background covered with little knots of pale blue flowers.

Lily walked towards the window. 'This is where my bed was,' she said. 'Under the window, right here. The first thing I did every day was pull back the curtains to see if the sun was shining. I was always ever so disappointed when it wasn't. Over there I had my table with the mirror on it, and my wardrobe was in the corner. Oh, yes, and my bookcase was just there.' She pointed. 'Behind the door.'

Every time the light from the phones died, they punched a key to spark them back into life.

Lily shook her head. 'I can't believe no one's been living here,' she murmured. 'No one's been living here since we moved away.'

'We've got to go, Lils,' said Rick. 'We need to get the bus home.'

Lily didn't answer.

'Lily, did you hear what I said?' He was getting impatient.

Ignoring him, all of a sudden Lily crouched down. Shining the phone under the window, she began to peer at the wall as though she was looking for something.

Exasperated, Rick snapped, 'What do you think you're doing now?'

'Just wait!' she hissed back. Her face broke into a smile. 'There it is!' she gasped.

'What?'

Lily glanced up at him and pointed to a spot low down on the wall. Sighing, Rick crouched and aimed the light from his phone at the place Lily showed him.

Two words had been written there in pencil. Very faint, but still just about clear enough to read.

'"Lily's bedroom".' Rick read them out loud. 'Did *you* write that?'

Lily nodded. 'When Mum told me we were moving, I didn't want to go. So I thought, "What can I do to make this my room forever?"'

'And you wrote, "Lily's bedroom"?' Rick said.

'Yeah. I wrote it on the wall behind the bed so Mum wouldn't see it. I knew if she did, she'd make me rub it off. But I was sure that one day, whoever had my room next would find it. It's like a message. Then they'd know it would never really be theirs.'

Rick nodded. 'And now it isn't anyone's.'

Lily shot him a look. 'Of course it's someone's,' she said. 'No one else is living here, so it's still mine. This whole house is still mine … **It always will be.'**

When Lily saw Danny, she was on her own. Rick and the other two Dixons had wanted to hang around at the shopping centre after school and Lily hadn't felt like it. She'd set off for Rick's house by herself, but halfway there, she'd decided not to go back straight away. The twins would be home and they didn't seem to leave her alone when she got in from school. She didn't always mind, but today she wasn't in the mood. She decided to head for the park and go back later.

Danny was there with some others from the Topz Gang, Dave, Josie and Paul. Paul was on crutches.

'Erm … hi,' said Danny.

'Hi,' Lily answered. Without waiting to be introduced

she looked at Paul and asked, 'What happened to you?'

'Long story,' Paul began. 'Actually it's not. It was all over very quickly. One minute I was leap-frogging, the next I was in agony. That's about it really.'

Lily simply nodded, as if it was something that happened every day. 'Is it hard to walk with those?' She indicated the crutches.

'Not really,' replied Paul. 'They're quite handy round puddles, too. You don't have to get your feet wet because you can just sort of swing yourself over them.'

'Or,' said Dave, 'you can *not* get your feet wet by just sort of stepping over them if you don't happen to have a pair of crutches.'

Paul thought for a moment. 'Well … yeah,' he agreed.

'So anyway, this is Lily,' said Danny. 'She was at the wedding last weekend.'

'Oh, yeah!' smiled Josie. 'It was your mum who got married, wasn't it?'

'Yup.' Lily didn't want to talk about the wedding. She glanced at the football Danny was holding in the crook of his arm. 'Am I interrupting your game?'

'No.' Danny shook his head. 'No, we haven't started.' He hesitated a moment, then, 'Why? Did you want to join in?'

'Not really, but thanks.'

There was an awkward silence. Josie had the feeling that Lily wanted to talk to Danny on his own.

'Give us the ball, then, Danny,' she said. 'Come over in a minute, yeah?'

Danny tossed the ball to her. She caught it and the three Topz wandered away.

'He's not seriously going to play football on crutches, is he, Danny?' Lily asked.

'Yeah, kind of,' Danny grinned.

'I'm sorry I couldn't talk long in the shop the other day,' she went on. 'It's difficult when Rick's there.'

'I know. It doesn't matter. How's it going at his house?'

'It's fine. It's good. But then he doesn't hate me. Well, not yet anyway.'

Danny smiled. 'I've been emailing Dad. We've been emailing each other.'

Lily didn't answer.

'Have you spoken to your mum yet?'

'She's been texting.' That's all Lily would say.

'Does she like it in New Zealand?'

Lily looked vaguely irritated. 'Yes – I think so. But that's not what I wanted to talk about.'

'OK.'

Danny waited.

'You don't seem that upset,' Lily began. 'I know Rick upset you with what he said, but you seem all right. You don't seem to mind that much that your dad's gone.'

'I *do* mind,' Danny said quickly. 'I mind a lot. I didn't want this to happen. I didn't want it to *be* like this. Mum's really down. It's just …'

'What?'

'It's just that I think sometimes stuff happens. And you don't really understand why and you can't always see the good part in it. But somehow you just have to believe that it'll turn out all right in the end.'

Lily gazed into Danny's face. 'You believe in God, don't you?'

'Erm …' For a moment, Danny was lost for words. Lily asked the most direct and unexpected questions.

'Rick told me,' she added. 'I told him it wasn't a reason not to like someone.'

'Thanks,' Danny spluttered.

'I wish *I* did,' Lily said. 'Believe in God, I mean. I kind of envy you in a way.'

This was not the conversation Danny was expecting. 'You don't have to envy me,' he replied hesitantly. 'God wants to be *everyone's* Friend. You just need to ask Him.'

'Do you talk to God about your dad?'

'Yeah. All the time.'

'Did you ask Him not to let your dad go away?' Lily persisted.

Danny wasn't sure how to answer. Finally, 'Yes, I did,' he said. 'And first of all I was angry when Dad got the job in Spain. I was angry with God because I thought He'd let everything get messed up. But … there's this verse in the Bible that basically says God only wants the best for us. So I have to believe that what's happened is for the best … don't I?'

Lily studied him for a moment. 'Yes,' she said. 'Yes, I suppose you do. Like I say, I really envy you.'

Nine

It was Saturday the next time Lily and Rick went to visit the cottage in Fursley. Rick didn't want to go so Lily had to persuade him. Mostly by not taking no for an answer.

'Where are you two off to, then?' Elaine asked.

'Just out for a bit,' said Rick.

'Well, I'll certainly be able to tell your mum you're no trouble, Lily,' Elaine smiled. 'I hardly see you. You're always out!'

'Is that all right?' Lily asked.

'Of course it is, darling. You go and enjoy yourself.' In some ways Elaine was quite pleased that Rick was spending time with someone who wasn't a Dixon. 'Just make sure you text me so I know what's going on. OK?'

'OK,' Lily replied.

It would never have occurred to Elaine that Lily and Rick were catching a bus out of Holly Hill. Rick was always off doing something or other with Dixons. Most days he was out of the house more than in it. But even if Elaine didn't know *precisely* where he was, she always knew he was somewhere around Holly Hill.

'I don't see why we can't just tell her where we're going,' Rick grumbled as they headed for the bus stop. 'She probably wouldn't even mind.'

'Because she's bound to tell Mum,' Lily shrugged. 'And I don't want Mum to know.' Then, 'Did you remember to pick up the torch?' she asked, and Rick knew there was no point trying to argue about it.

The bus dropped them off outside Fursley post office and five minutes later they were walking along Bailey Place. They made sure there was no one around to see them, then slipped in the cottage front gate and round the back to the kitchen window. The board was still dangling from its one nail.

'I don't even know what we're doing here,' Rick muttered when they'd both clambered inside.

'Don't you like adventures?' Lily asked.

'Of course I do but this is just some old house.'

'It's not just *some old house*,' Lily retorted. She took the torch Rick had pulled from his rucksack and made her way to the lounge. 'It's *my* house and we can see it better now we've got a torch. Anyway, it's a secret – which is why it's an adventure.'

That's when Lily saw it. An empty can of lemonade on the lounge floor near the fireplace, caught in the torch beam. She stopped dead.

'That wasn't here before.'

Rick peered at it. 'I dunno,' he shrugged. 'It might have been. It was pretty dark.'

'I'm telling you,' Lily snapped, 'that can wasn't here before.' She rounded on him suddenly. 'Is this you, Rick? Is this someone you know? Did you tell anyone about my house?'

'Oh, don't be stupid!' Rick scowled. 'Why would I do that?'

Lily watched him. He looked almost hurt. She *did* trust him but could she trust him completely? With a secret as big as this?

Turning away, she swept the torch around the room. Immediately her eyes widened.

It wasn't just an empty lemonade can that had found its way into the lounge since their last visit. Nearby, stashed neatly against the wall, was what looked like a folded blanket and a biscuit tin, with another can of lemonade perched on the top.

Lily knelt down to take a closer look. The can hadn't been opened, and when she picked up the tin and took off the lid, she found it was full of chocolate muffins. She glanced round at Rick.

'None of this was here,' she murmured. 'None of it.'

Rick nodded. 'Well, whoever's left it must be coming back. It looks like they've been getting supplies in.'

'But they can't,' said Lily. 'It's not their house.'

'It's not yours either, Lils,' replied Rick, raising his eyes. He was getting a little tired of this argument.

'It's more mine than theirs,' Lily muttered, 'and I don't care what you say.'

She started to put the lid back onto the tin when Rick asked, 'Anyway, what's that?'

Lily didn't look at him. 'What?'

'*That.*' Rick picked up the torch that she'd put down on the floor and pointed it at something lying on top of the folded rug. Lily hadn't noticed what was hidden under the biscuit tin.

Rick bent down and grabbed it. 'It's a notebook.'

In his hand he held an exercise book with a cover patterned with coloured circles. When he flipped it open, he could see in the torchlight that the actual cover was blue. Someone had taken the trouble to stick the brightly patterned paper over the top.

Lily stood next to him, gazing down at it. Rick passed her the torch so that he could flick through the pages. The notebook was practically full of handwriting. Almost certainly a child's handwriting. Very small and very neat. There were just a few pages at the back that were still empty.

'Looks like … poems or something,' he said.

The frown on Lily's face deepened. 'Poems? Someone's been in my house writing poems?'

'Yeah,' smirked Rick. 'Listen to this: *It's quiet,*' he read. '*Rain falls like the tears on my face. It's warm outside but the rain is cold as ice.* **Like the ice-cold tears in my heart.**'

Rick screwed up his face. 'Ice-cold tears? What's that all about?' he scoffed. 'You don't get ice-cold tears, do you? Tears are warm. And you don't cry with your heart. You cry with your eyes.'

Lily took the book. She shook her head. 'I don't think that's what it means,' she said. Her eyes scanned the rest of the poem. '*When I cry, my heart cries too,*' she read. '*But no one hears because no one's listening.*'

'What a load of rubbish!' Rick chuckled. 'I never did get poems.'

'This is sad,' Lily said. She read down the rest of the page. 'Whoever wrote it must have been *really* sad.'

Suddenly she snapped the book closed. 'Hold on to it,' she said, shoving it into Rick's hands. 'I'm going to take a look upstairs.'

'What for?'

'In case whoever's been in here has left anything else.' She turned briefly in the doorway. 'I'll be back in a minute.'

As soon as Lily had disappeared with the torch, darkness closed back into the lounge. Only the faintest, ragged chinks of light gleamed at the edges of the window.

Rick heard her feet on the stairs. He listened to the clunk of her footfalls on the bare floorboards as they echoed overhead while she went from room to room. Reaching into his pocket, he pulled out his phone and jabbed at it. The bluish light sprang out. He opened the book again. A different page this time.

'*This is my place. My space*,' he read aloud. '*My life. My strife. Not that there was much strife before you came. Most of the time you are the strife.*' He laughed. 'Whoever's written this stuff must be dead weird!' he called to Lily. 'And if you find them up there, you can tell them I said that! *Some days I don't care*,' he read on. '*But today I don't want you in my lair. You're everywhere. You're in my hair.*' Rick shrieked with laughter again. 'Lily! I think they've got headlice!'

There was no response. Then, 'Rick, come up here a minute!' Lily called.

'What's wrong?' No answer. Rick dropped the book on the floor. He shone the light from his phone in front of him and made his way upstairs.

'Lils?'

Lily wasn't in her own bedroom. She was in the one that had been her mum's. Rick followed the glow from the torchlight.

'What is it?' he asked.

Lily didn't answer. She just held out a plastic carrier bag. Rick took it and looked inside. There were packets of biscuits and crisps, more cans of lemonade, a torch and some batteries.

Lily swung their torch to shine through the open door of a built-in cupboard. In the cone of light, Rick saw the small pile of books, notebooks and a handful of pens.

'OK,' he said slowly. 'That's a bit freaky.'

'We didn't come in this room last week,' Lily said. 'First of all I was thinking maybe this stuff was here and we missed it. Maybe someone had been in here before us.' She shook her head. 'But there wasn't a way into the cottage before we came, Rick. It was all boarded up. We *made* the way in. Some kid must have found the loose board after we pulled it off the kitchen window.'

'We don't know it's a kid.'

'It's a kid's handwriting, Rick. I'm sure of it.'

'Well, if they've left this here,' Rick said, 'chances are they could be back any time.'

'Yeah,' Lily replied firmly. 'And that's when I'll tell them to take their stuff and get out.'

'Are you serious?' Rick dumped the carrier bag back in the cupboard with the books. 'We're not hanging around waiting for them to come back! It could be anyone. We don't know anything about them, Lily.'

Lily stared at him. 'Do the other Dixons know what a scaredy cat you are?'

The more Rick got to know Lily, the more he realised that she was one of the most infuriating people he'd ever met. She had this way of turning things around. All the time. Of making him do what he didn't want to do, with just a word or an expression on her face. Even just the look in her eyes.

'Besides,' Lily added without waiting for him to answer, 'we *do* know something about them. We know they write poetry.'

Rick shook his head; pressed his lips together. He was supposed to be looking after her. If Lily was staying, he'd have to stay, too. He knew there was no way he could get her to leave until she was ready to go.

'D'you know what I really don't get?' Rick grunted. 'Back at the hotel after your mum's wedding, you were terrified to go into that bedroom. You were so scared we'd be caught. Why aren't you scared here?'

'Why would I be?' Lily answered flatly. 'This is my house.

It's where I used to live. I belong here.'

She brushed past him, taking the torch with her.

'*Now* where are you going?' Rick demanded. He followed on behind.

'Downstairs. What does it look like?'

'If we get into trouble, this is *your* fault, Lily,' he said. 'It's nothing to do with me, it's all *you*. You got that?'

Back in the lounge, Lily swept the torch beam around, looking for the exercise book.

'Where did you put it?' she asked.

'Where did I put what?' Rick answered gruffly. 'What are you on about now?'

'The book of poems. You had it when I went upstairs.'

'It's on the floor. I dropped it when you called.' Rick looked down towards his feet. He was standing more or less in the same place where he'd been just before he'd stopped reading. He'd let the book fall. Right there. He'd heard it land on the floorboards.

So where was it?

Lily frowned at him. 'Maybe you took it up with you.'

'No, I didn't. It was here. I was reading some rubbish about "You're in my lair, you're everywhere, you're in my hair" – and then you called and I dropped it. *Right here.*'

There was a pause. Barely a fraction of a second.

Then, all of a sudden, the missing exercise book shot through the air from a dark corner of the room.

Rick couldn't lift his hands to protect himself because he never saw it coming. It smacked into his face.

'Rubbish, is it?' screeched a voice. 'How dare you! How dare you read my book! How dare you even **touch** it!' /

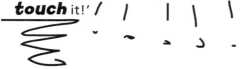

Ten

Hi Dad.

Danny's fingers tapped away at the computer keyboard.

I've decided to redesign my room. Are you any good at putting up shelves? Paul's dad does lots of stuff like that. Paul says they could almost build a whole new house from all the wood in all the shelves his dad has put up. Anyway, so I was wondering – I mean, only if you've got time when you come home – if you'd like to put up some shelves for me. I was thinking that I could move my bed under the window and put my desk against the wall where my bed is at the moment. Then if you could put up some shelves above my desk, I'd have loads of space to store all my school junk. And all within easy reach of my computer! What do you think?

I'm also going to sort out my cupboard. Mum says you can hardly see my clothes for all the rubbish. Well, it's what she calls rubbish. Some of it's really useful. Like my homemade Monopoly board. Do you remember that? Benny says there are some things you should keep forever because you never know when they might come in handy. My homemade Monopoly board's one of those things, I reckon. So I thought that if I sorted everything out, tidied it up and moved the furniture around, then all that would be left to do would be the shelves. I haven't told Mum yet. I thought I'd surprise her.

So, how's it going out there in Spain? Do you miss England? I think I'd miss England if I had to be in another country for as long as you've got to be there. Are you making lots of friends? Hope so. Don't want you to be lonely.

Going round to John's in a bit. He's got a new Grand Prix DVD. He says he wants to be a racing driver. Well, that's what he wants to be this month. Last month he wanted to be an airline pilot. And I think some time before that he wanted to be a fireman. John's finding it hard to make up his mind, I reckon. Although lately, I've been thinking it would be quite cool to be an astronaut. Way up in space looking back at the world. I sometimes wonder if that's how God sees it. The whole planet just floating in space.

There was a full moon last night. Really bright. It's weird thinking that Mum and I were looking at it from here in England, and the same moon would have been shining over Spain. Did you see the moon last night? Tell me if you did. How cool would that be if we were looking at the same thing at kind of the same time from different countries!

I've been praying for you, Dad. You should talk to God, too. That's something else we can do together while we're in different countries. God hears everyone. It doesn't matter where you are. You could ask Him to look after you over there and help you find another job back here. That's what I'm doing. He'll work everything out for us because that's what He's promised. I told that to Lily and do you know what she said? She said she envied me. She envied the way I believed in God and trusted Him to make everything OK somehow. But you know what, Dad? That's SO not a reason to be envious. Everyone can be friends with God because He wants us all to know Him. That includes you and me ... and Lily, too.

I wish Lily would talk to God. He'd help her, I know He would. She's finding it really hard with her mum getting married. No idea why she didn't want to go to New

Zealand on holiday with them. I'd love to have gone! Then she'd have been much more part of it. She didn't want to be a bridesmaid either. Lily's kind of strange in a way but I really like her. Anyway, I know I go on about it, Dad, but please talk to God. He'll like that.

Better stop now and head over to John's. Do you know when you're coming home for a visit yet? Hope it's soon. We miss you. Although Mum did say last night that she doesn't miss the extra washing. Seriously though, she really misses you. Talks about you all the time. Not just to me, to everybody. You must be the most talked about dad in Holly Hill.

If the moon's up tonight, look at it. I'll be looking, too. Love you, Dad.

Danny xx

PS. Benny wants me to ask you if you've had a Spanish omelette yet.

Hi Danny.

Thanks for your email. Yes, I was looking at the moon last night and, oddly enough, I wondered if you and your mum could see it, too! It was a very hot day here yesterday, and the night sky was so clear and full of stars. Quite beautiful. God should be very proud. Hot today, too, which should mean another clear night, so I'll look out for the moon again and know that you're watching it with me. As you say, amazing that we can be in different countries but seeing exactly the same thing. There you are, you see. I'm not so far away after all.

Making a few friends, yes. Of course it helps being here with your uncle. He's introduced me to a lot of people already and they're all very nice and very interested in my family and what I do at home. If you think Mum's talking about me a lot, that's nothing compared to all the time I'm spending talking about the two of you. It's quite a surprise I'm getting any work done at all! And on the talking front, it also helps that there are lots of English people working here. And so many Spanish people speak really good English, too. So I'm being a bit lazy. So far I don't think my Spanish has improved at all.

I'll be honest, Danny, I'm not a natural when it comes to putting up shelves. Or any DIY come to that. You probably don't remember but I did once try to put a shelf up in the bathroom. It looked wonderful, too, until Mum started to put things on it. Came off the wall completely bringing two large lumps of plaster with it. That's why we've now got that little cabinet on the floor by the bath. Mum's never asked me to put up a shelf since then. She wasn't best pleased. Can't say I blame her, mind. She was having a bath when it came down. Missed her by inches. Created quite a splash, too. Soaked the curtains as I remember. Having said that, I think sorting out your room is an excellent idea. Once you've moved your desk you might find there's room for a little bookcase next to it. Could be a safer way to store your things than on one of my shelves.

We're going out for a meal tonight. It's your uncle's birthday and he wants to try a new restaurant that's just opened in town. Tell Benny that if Spanish omelette's on the menu, then that's what I'll have. And I'll make sure to eat it with a big salad so you can tell your mum I'm looking after myself.

Not sure exactly which weekend I'll be able to get home yet. But three or four weeks at the most now, Danny.

And I'll join you and Mum tonight for a spot of moon-gazing. Looking forward to it.

Lots of love

Dad x

Hi Dad.

Just back from John's. His Grand Prix DVD's really cool. I can see why he wants to be a racing driver. Looks like so much fun. Maybe we could go to a Grand Prix some time. Or some other sort of car racing. Either that or we could just watch it on TV together. We could have chips and hot dogs and pretend we're there for real. Still think I'd rather be an astronaut than a racing driver, though. What about you?

Gotta go. Hope you find a Spanish omelette. Miss you. See you later at the moon.

Lots of love
Danny xx

Eleven

For an instant, Rick and Lily stood in the lounge of the empty house, frozen in terror. Rick was so stunned he hardly even felt the sting of the exercise book as it swiped across his skin. That came afterwards. After the girl who had screeched at them had stepped out from the shadows. She shone a torch right into their faces.

Lily squinted. She couldn't see a thing with the light full in her eyes. She certainly couldn't make out who had just thrown the book. Not properly. She twisted Rick's torch to glare the beam at the girl in front of them.

'How dare *we*?' she snarled. 'How dare *you*! This is *my* house. Mine! And as far as I can see, that makes *you* a trespasser!'

The three children stared at each other. No one moved.

Then the girl, who was small for her thirteen years with a pointed chin and blonde, bobbed hair, lowered her torch and stepped forward to pick up her book. But Rick was too quick for her. He snatched it away before she could reach it.

'Oh no, you don't,' he growled. 'You don't get to chuck your book at me and then have it back.'

'And you don't get to read it and say it's rubbish!' the girl snapped. 'Now, give it to me!'

'No!'

The girl made a grab for it, but Rick whirled it away. 'It's not yours, *give* it to me!'

'Oh, just give it back to her, Rick,' muttered Lily.

Rick scowled at her. 'What? Why?'

'Because the book doesn't matter,' Lily answered.

'What matters is who she is and why she's in my house.'
'It's not *your* house,' mumbled the girl.

'It used to be,' Lily retorted. 'And I don't see anyone else living here now, so if you ask me that makes it *still* mine. At least more mine than yours.'

The girl studied Lily in the torchlight. 'Did you really used to live here?' she asked.

'Well, I'm not going to say I did if I didn't, am I?' She turned on Rick. 'Just give her back the book, Rick!'

Rick glanced at Lily. His eyes held a glint of fury. But he clenched his teeth together and tossed the book to the floor at the girl's feet. Slowly, without lowering the torch from their faces, the girl bent down and picked it up.

'Now, what are you doing here?' Lily demanded. 'When we first came here, no one had been in this house. No one had been in it for ages, far as we could tell. And none of your stuff was here, I'm sure of it. So how come you're here now?'

The girl hesitated. 'I saw you,' she said finally.

'What do you mean?' Lily frowned.

'Last week. I saw you go round the back of the house. I followed you.'

'You couldn't have done.' Lily shook her head. 'There was no one around. We were keeping a lookout.'

'Well, you're not very good at it, then, because I was watching you from the trees by the footpath. I was there with my bike.' As if to prove what she was saying, the girl continued, 'You spoke to that woman first. You asked what had happened to the houses and she told you about the new road. When you said you were going to try and get in I thought I'd see if you did it. I come past here all the time, but I never thought about doing that 'til I overheard you. I watched you pull the board down. I had to go then but I came back the next day.'

Lily stared at her. 'So you just decided to move in?'

'I haven't *moved* in.' The girl looked cross again. 'I've got a home, you know. It's just … sometimes these days, I need my own space. I thought this could be it.'

'But it's not yours,' Lily argued.

'It's not yours either!'

'That's what I've been trying to tell her,' muttered Rick. Lily jabbed her elbow hard into him.

'Ow!' he yelled angrily. 'What was that for?'

'You're supposed to be backing me up, Rick!' Lily took a step towards the girl, still shining the torch full in her face. 'Why do you need more space anyway? Isn't your own house big enough or something?'

The girl shrugged. 'Of course it's big enough. I mean, we all fit, if that's what you mean. It's just … it's just that we used to fit better. When it was just Mum and me.'

Instantly the scowl on Lily's face switched to an expression of surprise.

'What do you mean?' she asked.

'I've got a stepbrother now. Well, and a stepdad obviously. But my stepbrother's only little. He doesn't even start school 'til next term. He stays with us one week then goes to his mum the next; then he comes back to us for a week again, and on and on. And the weeks he's with us, he's the one who seems to take up all the space. He gets everywhere and he doesn't give me any peace! I mean, don't get me wrong,' she added, a fond half-smile crossing her face, 'he is gorgeous. Always making me laugh. It's just that sometimes I want to be left alone. When I saw you climb in here I thought I could come here, too. Just when I need to get away from him.'

Lily nodded slowly. 'What's his name?'

'Danny,' said the girl.

'Ha!' smiled Lily. 'I've got a friend called Danny!'

Rick curled his lip. 'Hardly a friend.'

'Yes, he is,' answered Lily firmly. 'He's my friend. I'm Lily, by the way, and this is Rick. And Rick didn't mean what he said about your poems,' she added quickly, without looking at him. 'We only read a little bit, honestly. I think your writing's lovely.'

The girl gave another half-smile. 'I'm Hazel. And I'm sorry if you thought I was trespassing. I didn't think you'd mind. I didn't even know if you'd be back.'

'What? Stay away from my own house?' Lily grinned. 'Not a chance!'

Rick was starting to fidget. 'I think we should get going now, Lils.'

'Why?' Lily replied. 'We've hardly been here any time.'

'I know, but Mum'll start to wonder where we are.'

'We'll get back for lunchtime. It'll be fine.'

But Rick had had enough. Lily had been pushing him around ever since her mum had gone away, and she just kept doing it. Now she was doing it in front of Hazel. He wasn't going to take it any more.

'No, Lily, we're going.' There was an edge to his voice.

'OK,' Lily sighed. 'If you're so anxious to get back, then go home. No one's stopping you, you've got your bus ticket.'

'I can't go without you, can I?' he said. 'I'm *supposed* to be looking after you.'

'Yes, so you keep saying! But in case you haven't noticed, Rick, I don't need looking after! Mum obviously didn't think I needed looking after, did she, or she wouldn't have left me with you!'

Rick's jaw dropped. How could Lily speak to him like that? After everything he'd tried to do? After he'd gone along with everything she wanted?

Furious, he shoved past her and stormed down the hall to the kitchen.

'Don't you dare tell anyone where I am!' Lily yelled after him. 'If anyone in Holly Hill finds out about this place I'll *know* it was you!'

No answer. Rick was gone.

Hazel stood awkwardly in the lounge with Lily. 'You two don't like each other much.'

'Yes, we do,' Lily replied quietly. 'He's all right really. He just makes me so mad. He doesn't understand.'

'Doesn't understand what?' Hazel asked.

'Anything,' Lily mumbled. 'Anything about me.' Her eyes flicked to Hazel's face. 'I think you might, though. I'm like you, d'you know that?'

'How do you mean?'

'I've got a stepdad.'

Lily and Hazel talked as if they'd known each other for ages. Lily told her everything. How she'd never known her dad because he'd left before she was born; about liking Andy but not wanting him to be her stepdad; about refusing to be a bridesmaid for her mum and go away on the honeymoon.

'I just don't want this,' Lily said, 'and Mum doesn't get it. No one gets it.'

'Do *you*?' Hazel asked. 'Do you know why you feel like you do?'

'I think so,' Lily nodded. 'It's just if I told Mum, it would sound stupid. She'd think I was being an idiot, I know she would.' She smiled. 'She calls me a puzzle. Rick did once, too. I don't know, maybe I am.'

Hazel looked thoughtful. 'The thing is, I don't mind having a stepdad,' she said. 'I'm lucky. He's really nice and he's really good to me and Mum. And I love Danny, but you know what little kids are like. They get everywhere! I just need to get away from him sometimes.' She paused. 'I did know my dad, Lily. I loved him, too. Lots and lots. But he died when I was nine. I couldn't really talk about it. I didn't know how, I suppose. Mum was really worried I was bottling it all up. I had to go to the doctor and everything. But I still couldn't really tell anyone how I felt. Not back then when it had just happened. So that's when I started writing poems. They weren't meant for anyone to read. They just helped *me*. I could describe how I was feeling so much better when I wrote it down.'

Lily gazed at her. 'I'm sorry about your dad.'

'It's fine. What I'm trying to say,' Hazel continued quickly, 'is that if you're having a hard time, try writing it down. Make some poems out of it, maybe. It might help you sort your head out a bit like it did me. I don't write about my dad so much any more,' she added. 'I think about him a lot but I write about other things, too. You should come here and write your poems. It can be your special place. I thought I could do some writing here, too, but … well, I won't if you don't want me to.'

'No!' Lily grabbed her hand. 'No, of course I want you to! I'm sorry I said all that stuff before. You're not a trespasser at all! You can come here whenever you want.'

The girls switched off their torches to save the batteries and talked on in the semi-darkness. It was Rick's text bleeping into Lily's phone that interrupted them:

In park. Meet me here by 2. Need 2 go home 2gether or Mum will guess something up.

Lily glanced at the time on the screen.

'It's nearly one,' she said. 'I think there's a bus at twenty past. I'd better go.'

'We could meet here again if you like,' suggested Hazel.

'What about next Saturday? Same time?'

Lily's face lit up. 'Yeah!' she beamed. 'Yeah, next Saturday'll be great! I won't bring Rick. He doesn't want to come over here anyway.'

Hazel smiled back at her. 'See you, then, Lily.'

'Yeah,' Lily said again. 'See you, Hazel.'

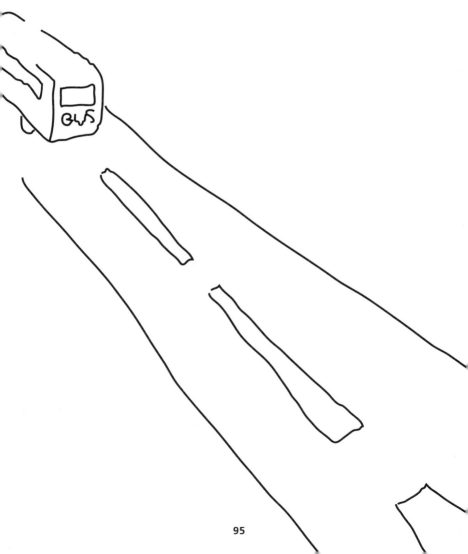

Twelve

For a few days after meeting Hazel at the cottage, Rick didn't talk to Lily much. He was still angry. Elaine was worried.

'Come on, Rick, out with it?' she kept asking. 'What's gone on between you two?'

'Nothing, Mum,' Rick snapped. 'Stop asking. We're fine. It's all fine.'

Elaine sighed. 'Oh dear. Honestly, you two can be worse than the twins.'

Lily didn't seem to care. But then it wasn't Rick she particularly wanted to talk to. It was Danny. Hazel had spoken to her about something – shown her something – and she was desperate to tell him. Lily didn't know where Danny lived and she certainly didn't want to ask Rick. But surely she'd see him around; walking home from school, in the park, at the shopping centre.

Only there was no sign of him. Day after day. It was as if he'd vanished off the face of the planet.

Until Friday. The day before Lily was due to go back to Fursley to meet Hazel again. That's when she spotted him coming out of the supermarket.

'Danny!'

Danny turned his head and saw Lily running towards him. So did the girl who was with him.

'Hi, Lily,' Danny said. Lily stopped, breathless, in front of him. 'Are you OK? What's up?'

'I've been looking for you everywhere,' she puffed. 'Every day! Where have you been?'

'Erm … school mainly,' he said, a little uncomfortably. 'This is Sarah,' he added, indicating the girl next to him.

'Hi, Sarah,' said Lily. 'I've seen you around. Are you a Topz, too?'

Sarah nodded but before she could speak, Lily had already begun again. 'Danny, could I talk to you?'

'Yeah, sure,' Danny answered. He still felt awkward. 'Now?'

'If you've got a minute. Well – maybe more than a minute.'

'Sure,' Danny said again. He glanced at Sarah. He didn't know if Lily would mind someone else hearing what she had to say or not, but he guessed she would. 'I'll see you at youth club later then, Sarah. Is that all right?'

Sarah wondered what was going on – what could be so important – and Danny thought she looked a little put out. But she took the hint and left them on their own.

'Sorry,' said Lily. 'I didn't mean to interrupt, it's just I've been dying to tell you something. Several things actually. And there's something I want to read to you, too.'

They wandered through the lines of shops, then sat on the bench outside the baker's.

'Hazel's incredible, Danny!' Lily bubbled. 'You'd really like her. She's a bit older than us but she's not bossy or full of herself or anything. And she understands what it's like to be you and me, because *she's* like us, too! What I mean is she lost her dad – and she's even got a stepdad now, which makes her *exactly* like me! Well, not totally exactly, I suppose, because she has a stepbrother as well. He's only tiny and you'll never guess what he's called!'

Danny looked at Lily, a little bewildered. Since Sarah had gone, she hadn't stopped talking. Even now, she didn't give him time to answer.

'Danny! Hazel's stepbrother's called Danny! Isn't that weird? I told her I had a friend called Danny.

Anyway she's got lots of pictures of him on her phone and he's gorgeous. Really smiley. Not like Rick's little sisters. Honestly, Danny, they do so much whinging, I'm not surprised Rick gets fed up with them! But do you know what Hazel does? She writes poems. I've read some of them and they're so beautiful. She started writing them when her dad died because she found it easier writing about how she felt than talking about it. She told me that's what I should do, too. Write about how I'm feeling – you know, about Mum and Andy and us being all together as a family. And I was thinking that maybe you could do that as well. You could write poems about your dad having to go away to work; about how it made you feel angry and sad; about how you miss him. You could do that, couldn't you, Danny? It might help you like it helped Hazel.'

Finally Lily stopped talking. She stared at Danny intently, waiting for him to answer.

'I'm not sure,' Danny said. 'I don't know that I'd be any good at writing poetry.'

'It doesn't matter!' Lily cried instantly, almost as if she'd known what he'd say. 'It's not meant for anyone to read. Not unless you *want* someone to read it. It's just meant to help you ... "express yourself". That's what Hazel says and that's why she does it.'

'And that's cool,' Danny nodded. He didn't want to sound as though he wasn't interested. 'It's just that ... well, I usually talk to *God* about how I feel. Even if I find it hard talking to my mates, I can still let God know what's going on. I mean, I can be really angry about something, but when I tell Him ... it helps.'

A smile began to spread across Lily's face.
'You could write poems, too, though, Danny.'

Without pausing for breath, she gabbled on.

'And that's the other thing I wanted to tell you about Hazel. She reads loads! She just loves books. Not just poetry books, but all sorts of books. Some of them are quite hard and grown up. I don't think I'd understand them, but *she* does. She must be so clever. But do you know what her favourite book is? It's the Bible, Danny! She's read lots of it, just like you have, and she loves it. She says it inspires her with her own writing more than anything else because it's so exciting and mysterious. I couldn't believe it when she told me that! Not after meeting you at Mum's wedding as well! I don't know if she's asked God to be her friend or anything. Not like you have. But she loves reading about Him. She showed me her Bible and where to find the book in it called Psalms. They're like poems, aren't they, the Psalms?

'And then this amazing thing happened! I told her about you and how you'd said there was a verse in the Bible that says God only wants the best for us – and do you know what she said? She said, "I think I know the one he means!" And she flipped through and found this verse that sounds just like what you were talking about! She wrote it down for me.'

Lily fished in her pocket and pulled out a piece of paper. She unfolded it quickly and showed it to Danny. He read the small, neat handwriting: *We know that in all things God works for good with those who love him ... (Romans 8:28)*. He was almost as amazed as Lily.

'Yeah,' he gulped. 'Yeah, that's the verse. That's the one I meant. It's the one that's helped me more than anything with Dad going away.'

Lily practically whooped with delight. 'Didn't I tell you Hazel's incredible? She knew! I mean, the Bible's long – really, really long – and she still knew where to find this verse!' She paused and gave a little shrug. 'And I think maybe God meant me to meet her.'

At that, Danny's eyes sparkled. 'I'd like to meet her, too. Does she live in Holly Hill?'

Lily glanced down; fiddled with her fingers. 'Erm … no. I was just out somewhere with Rick and we sort bumped into each other.'

'Where was that?'

'Oh, I don't know,' she replied impatiently. 'Somewhere or other. I just had to wait all week to tell you because I couldn't find you. Anyway listen, Danny, there's one more thing.' Lily wasn't going to give him the chance to ask any more questions. She went to her other pocket and pulled out another piece of folded paper. 'I did what Hazel told me to. I wrote a poem. I haven't shown it to anyone else and I'm not going to, but … I sort of want to read it to you. It was really helpful reading some of Hazel's poems, so I thought if I read you mine, you might be able to write your own, too. It's not very long. Would you mind?'

Danny shook his head. Lily was so excited and he didn't want to let her down. It did feel a little weird; sitting on a bench in the shopping centre, listening to a poem, while a constant stream of people ambled past.

Lily read quietly. Only Danny could hear. None of the passers-by took any notice.

Mum calls me a puzzle.
I suppose I am.
I don't do it on purpose
I just don't always know
how to say what's going on.
Why can't people understand
without me having to explain?
Why do people need to HEAR what I'm feeling
and why I'm feeling it?
Maybe they're the puzzles,
not me.
Maybe they're puzzles with a piece missing.
The piece that lets them look in my eyes
and know that I'm so scared.

My mum loved me when it was just me.
But now it's Andy too.
And I don't know if there's enough love
for both of us.

Lily pursed her lips. She felt awkward. Embarrassed now she'd read the words aloud.

'Told you it wasn't very long,' she mumbled. She held the piece of paper out to him. 'You can keep it if you want. But you mustn't show it to anyone. Not ever.'

Danny blinked at her. 'Of course I won't. That's a really good poem, Lily.'

She tossed her head. She seemed irritated. 'You don't have to say it's good. The point isn't about it being good. The point is it says what I feel. And you could write poems that say what *you* feel. You don't have to say it's good, Danny.'

Lily gave a brief smile. A sad smile, Danny thought. Then, before he could stop her, she was on her feet and hurrying away.

'Lily, wait!'

Danny watched as she disappeared out of sight.

He knew he didn't have to say the poem was good. He'd said it because that was how he felt.

Danny thought Lily's poem was beautiful.

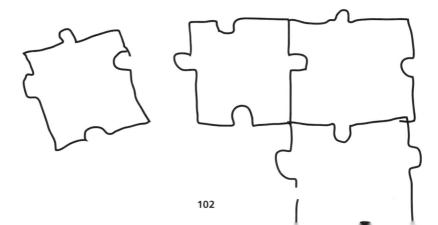

Thirteen

Hi Dad.

Mum just told me! You're coming home to visit next Saturday! That's SO cool! She says you might even be staying longer than just for the weekend. Maybe even the whole week! There's football on down at the playing fields next Sunday afternoon. We could go and watch if you like. Or we could stay in and watch TV. Or we could just go for a drive or something. If you say what you want to do then we'll do it. Mum's even talking about doing a cooked breakfast to celebrate on Sunday morning! And you know Mum NEVER does cooked breakfasts! That's how special you coming home is!

It's funny really because Saturday's when Lily's mum gets back from New Zealand, too. Lily doesn't seem very excited, though. She's quite unusual Lily is. I'm glad I got to meet her.

But **I'm** excited that **you're** coming home, Dad. I'll be able to show you my spider project. It's not finished yet. I don't have to give it in 'til after half term. But I've found some REALLY gross pictures on the internet. You'll love them!

I know it's crazy, but do you know what I'm really looking forward to? Standing outside the flats in the dark, side by side with you, watching the moon.

SEE YOU SATURDAY, DAD!!
Loads of love
Danny xx

103

'Lily's absolutely fine, Denise,' Elaine said into the phone. 'I'm afraid she's just out again, as usual.'

Elaine heard Denise sigh. 'She still doesn't want to talk to me, does she?'

'It's not that,' Elaine answered. She felt uncomfortable. Today Lily *was* out. But sometimes Denise had rung from New Zealand and Lily had looked at Elaine and pleaded with her eyes, 'Please don't make me talk to her.'

'By the time you get home, it'll all be fine, Denise,' Elaine went on.

'But we're home at the weekend,' Denise worried. 'She hasn't spoken to me the whole time I've been away. Supposing she still won't when I get back?'

'Oh, of course she will!' Elaine did her best to make Lily's mum feel better. 'It's been a big adjustment for her. I think she really regrets not going on holiday with you. So perhaps she thinks that if she talks to you on the phone, she'll just get even more upset.'

Denise didn't sound convinced. 'Perhaps you're right. I've had the odd text back from her, I suppose. Just a few words here and there. But … she is all right, isn't she, Elaine?'

'She's fine. Seriously, Denise, you've got to stop worrying. You're going to spoil what's left of your holiday. And she and Rick have been getting on like a house on fire. Most of the time anyway. They've had a few ups and downs but then they're kids. You've got to expect it, haven't you? I'm sure I was getting into endless scraps when I was their age. Weren't you?'

Lily sat on a swing in the park after school, slowly rocking herself backwards and forwards. In the distance, Rick kicked a football around with the other two Dixons. She half watched them; half gazed into space.

She'd had two texts from her mum that day. The first: *See u Saturday Lil. Have missed u loads!* The second: *Love u darling. See u soon.*

Lily hadn't replied to either of them. She didn't know what to say so how could she say anything?

There was something in her head. A thought. An idea. A feeling, perhaps. It was hard to pin it down. When Lily tried to focus on it, it seemed to shift like the movement of the swing.

She stopped rocking and reached for her school bag. There was a notebook and a pen inside. She took them out and flipped to a blank page. She started to write.

What are feelings anyway?
Things that come and live inside you
when you didn't invite them to.
Things that upset your day.
Or they can make you happy for no reason.
Then sometimes they let you stay happy
until a sad feeling sneaks in and
takes the happy feeling away again.
What would it be like not to have feelings?
I suppose that would be worse.
This feeling I have today makes me want to fidget.
I can't sit still.
I don't want to sit still.
There's something I think I need to do.
But if I did, it would shock everyone!
They'd stand around and raise their eyes

and shake their heads.
They'd say,
'Bad Lily!'
'Ungrateful Lily!'
They wouldn't try and understand.
They'd just feel sorry for Mum.
But if you're not sure of something
isn't it better to let it go completely
than wait around to find out
that you're right?
If Mum loves Andy now and not me
I don't want to see it.
I don't want to know it.
I don't want to be here at all.
And there's somewhere else I could go.

Rick ran up, breathing heavily. There was mud down one side of his trousers.

Lily hastily shut the notebook and thrust it back in her bag. 'Tch tch!' she tutted, nodding her head at the mud. 'Your mum's not going to be happy.'

Rick glanced down. 'It'll brush off.'

'Where are Kevin and Clyde?' Lily asked.

'Gone home,' Rick said. 'Shall we head back, too?'

'In a minute.'

Rick plonked himself down onto the swing next to her. 'You should play football, Lils,' he said.

'Why would I want to do that?'

'It's a laugh.'

Lily gave him a sideways glance. 'Do I look like I want to get covered in mud?'

'That is such a *girl* thing to say,' Rick grinned. 'Anyway, you don't *always* end up covered in mud.'

Again, Lily looked at him. '*You* do.'

Rick sniffed and started to rub at the brown and green stains on his trousers.

Lily watched him for a moment. 'Rick?' she asked. 'Do you still trust me?'

'Oh, not this again!' Rick shook his head. 'You know I do but I'm not doing any more stuff with my eyes closed, all right?'

'So if I said I was going to do something because it was for the best, would you let me do it?'

Rick's eyes narrowed. 'What are you getting at?'

'Mum and Andy. They've got a new life. They don't need me any more.'

'Lils,' Rick sighed, 'they're practically on their way home. Don't start all this now. What's the point?'

Lily started to rock on the swing again. 'There's a big point,' she said. 'Because I think I've worked it out. What to do, I mean.'

Rick clenched his teeth. 'But you don't have to do anything, do you? They're coming home. You didn't want them to go and now it's all over and they're coming back again. You should be happy, not "working out what to do".'

Lily stared at him.

'Bad Lily!'

'Ungrateful Lily!'

'D'you know,' Rick grumbled, shaking his head, 'I feel sorry for your mum sometimes.'

Lily didn't take her eyes off him.

They wouldn't try and understand.

They'd just feel sorry for Mum.

It was as if Rick had read her poem.

'Anyway, I've decided,' Lily murmured. 'I've got somewhere else I can go and I don't care what you think.'

'Well, why are you telling me, then?' Rick was exasperated. He couldn't hide it.

'Because I thought I should tell someone and I thought you might be interested. I thought you might *care*! Huh! Got that wrong.'

Lily stood up from the swing, slung her rucksack moodily across one shoulder and started to walk away.

'Lils, wait! Come back a minute!' Rick called.

Lily didn't turn round; didn't stop walking.

Fourteen

Danny's mum was hoovering on Saturday morning when Rick turned up at the flat. She almost didn't hear the buzzer.

'No, Danny's not here at the moment,' she said. She was more than a little surprised to see the Dixons boy standing there. 'He's gone out to do some errands for me. He'll be home in a little while.'

Rick fidgeted. 'I need to see him. It's really important.'

'Well, as I say,' Danny's mum repeated, 'he'll be home in a little while. Come back later if you need to see him that badly.'

She spoke firmly. She didn't trust this boy an inch.

'It's just …' Rick picked at his thumbnail. 'Oh, never mind.' He shook his head and started to turn away.

Danny's mum watched him. The boy seemed upset. Almost distressed.

'Wait a minute, Rick,' she said. 'What's the problem?'

Rick half turned towards her. 'I just need his help,' he mumbled. 'It doesn't matter.'

Danny's mum folded her arms and studied him. 'Oh, yes? And why do you need my Danny's help all of a sudden? Why can't your Dixons mates help you out?'

Rick shrugged miserably. 'They can't this time, that's all. It's got to be Danny.'

Danny's mum sucked in a breath and let it out slowly. 'All right. He's gone to the corner shop for a few things. He didn't leave long ago. If you hurry you'll probably still catch him there. And Rick,' she added sternly, 'if you're out to make any kind of trouble, then I shall be the one knocking on *your* door.'

'There won't be any trouble, honest,' Rick muttered. 'And … thanks.'

Outside the flats, Rick ran. This must be the way Danny walked to the corner shop. He knew it was the way the Topz boy walked to the park. If Danny was on his way back, he'd be bound to meet him.

Still running, Rick turned left at the junction and headed along the main street. The corner shop was soon in sight. But there was no sign of Danny. As Rick reached the shop doorway, a man came out holding a carrier bag. Rick almost barged into him in his hurry to get inside.

'Oi!' grunted the man. 'Watch where you're going!'

Rick took no notice. All he wanted to do was to find Danny. He marched in and quickly scanned the first aisle. Still no sign. Danny wasn't in the second one either. Where was he? He *had* to be in here somewhere, didn't he?

Rick turned into the third aisle. There!

'Danny!'

Danny's head whipped round. He almost dropped the box of soap powder he'd picked up. When he saw Rick his heart sank. He put the box into his basket with the rest of the shopping.

'What do *you* want?' he sighed.

'Can you finish shopping later?' Rick said. 'I really need your help.'

Danny stared at him. Since when did Dixons come to Topz for help? It was a trick, it must be. Some sort of stupid prank Rick was playing with Kevin and Clyde.

'No, I've got to get this back to Mum now. She's waiting. Dad's coming home today.'

Danny went to brush past him but Rick stood in his way.

'Yeah?' he said. 'Well, Lily's mum's coming home today, too. She's on the way from the airport. She could be here in an hour. Only there's just one problem. Lily's gone.'

Danny frowned. 'What do you mean "gone"?'

'Missing. Vanished. We got up this morning and she'd cleared out. Taken all her stuff and everything. Mum's going mad. She thought Lily might have gone back to her own house but she went round there and nothing. I mean, what's she going to say when Lily's mum turns up and Lily's not here?' He paused; swallowed. 'I told her I'd find her. I told her I'd bring her back.'

This wasn't a prank. Danny stared into Rick's face. He could see how grey he looked; how agitated. He knew the Dixons boy was telling the truth.

'So you haven't seen her since yesterday?' Danny's mind whirled. 'You're sure?'

Rick nodded his head.

'And she didn't say anything to you last night? You had no idea she was thinking of going off?'

'No ...' Rick trailed off. He looked even more wretched.

'What?' Danny demanded. 'What, Rick? If you know something, you've got to tell me.'

Rick gulped hard. 'She did say something a few days ago. Something about her mum and Andy not needing her any more so she was going to go somewhere else because she could.'

'What?' Danny eyes grew wider by the second. 'Didn't you tell her not to? Didn't you tell her she was being silly?'

'Yes ... No ... I don't know, I wasn't really listening! She just goes on and on sometimes. She's really been winding me up. She's says crazy stuff.'

Danny looked at him, disbelieving, for another instant. Then he shoved past.

'No, Danny, wait!' snapped Rick. 'I think I know where she is … In fact I'm sure I know where she is.'

Danny turned. 'Then why are you here?' he growled. 'Why aren't you there getting her back?'

Rick hung his head. 'There wouldn't be any point,' he said. 'She's never going to listen to me. That's why I had to find you.' He raised his eyes to meet Danny's. 'Lily likes you, Danny. She likes you a lot. If anyone can get her to come back – it's you.'

Danny paid for the shopping and the two boys marched quickly back to Danny's flat.

'You should have told your mum, Rick,' muttered Danny. 'You should have told her where Lily's gone.'

'I couldn't, could I? If she knew I'd been going back to Lily's old house with her, I'd have been in dead trouble. She'd have grounded me for a year! I was supposed to be looking after her, not going off with her on the bus to weird places I've never been to before.'

'Well, if you get grounded that's *your* problem, isn't it?' Danny answered. 'This is all your fault. If you hadn't agreed to go with her in the first place, she'd probably never have gone back there. We've got to tell your mum where you think she is.'

Rick stopped. 'No! We'll just go there now. You can talk to her, get her to come back and then no one ever needs to know.'

Danny rounded on him. 'I think Lily's mum's going to need to know, Rick. You said she's going to be here in an hour. There's no way we'll get to Fursley and back *and* persuade Lily to come home before then. No way.'

Rick clasped his hands together and clamped them

desperately to his forehead. 'I know! What are we going to do?'

Danny sighed; he thought quickly. 'We're going to go home and give my mum the shopping. Then we're going to go round to your house and tell your mum everything. And then, Rick,' he said, walking away, 'we're going to get the bus to Fursley. Now let's go.'

There was something else Danny needed to do when he dropped the shopping off. Something he needed to fetch from his bedroom to take with him to give to Rick's mum.

Rick was wrong. Lily wasn't likely to come back to Holly Hill just because Danny asked her to. Danny knew that. The only person she'd come back for was her mum. And if her mum was going to persuade her that everything was all right – that everything would work out for the best – then she'd need to be able to solve her Lily puzzle.

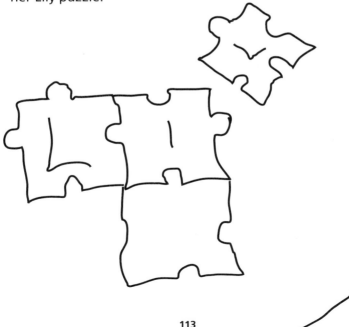

Fifteen

Lily sat on the floor under the window in torch lit darkness. She watched dust dance in the beam of light. She breathed in the musty air of her bedroom in Bailey Place while she munched on an apple. Every crunch was so loud in the stillness. Loud enough to scare away any rats, she thought.

Hazel might come later. They could spend the afternoon reading books and writing poems.

When Lily heard noises in the kitchen and the sound of footsteps on the stairs, she stood up expectantly.

Danny stepped into the doorway.

Lily's smile froze.

'What are you doing here?' she said quietly. 'I thought you were Hazel. How did you know where I was?'

'Rick guessed.'

'Well, that's weird, isn't it? I didn't think he was listening.' Lily turned away and shook her head. 'I told him not to tell anyone about this place. I should have known I couldn't trust him. Is he here?'

Danny nodded. 'He's outside. He was worried about you.'

Lily snorted. 'No, he wasn't! Rick only worries about himself. He's worried that *he'll* get in trouble because he knows he shouldn't have let me come here. I'm right, aren't I?'

Danny sighed. He wasn't going to lie. 'I dunno. Partly. But, do you remember what I told you? Do you remember that Bible verse? However things happen, Lily, God can work them out for the best. I'm glad Rick told me where you are. It was the right thing to do.'

Lily turned. 'Why? So you can persuade me to go home? Well, I'm not going to, so you may as well leave. *This* is my home now. It used to be once and it can be again.'

Danny shone his torch around the room. 'It's a bit … dark,' he said.

'That's what the torches are for, silly,' Lily muttered. Then, 'I don't want Rick to come in, but you can stay for a bit if you want to. I'm waiting for Hazel. She might come over later. You could meet her.'

'I'd like that.' Danny smiled. 'I'll stay.'

Lily's Auntie Mandy picked Denise and Andy up from the airport and drove them home. As soon as their bags were unloaded and indoors, Denise got into her own car and drove round to Rick's house.

Elaine was almost in tears when she opened the front door. 'I'm so sorry, Denise,' she gulped. She could hardly get the words out. 'Lily's fine. Rick's texted and she's absolutely fine. She's just … not here.'

'She's *where*?' Denise gasped when Elaine told her. 'Why?'

'I don't know exactly,' sniffed Elaine. 'But that boy, Danny, he's with her, too. And …' Her voice trailed off as she fished for something in her pocket. 'He told me to give you this.'

She held out a folded piece of paper. Denise looked at it questioningly.

'I don't know what it is,' Elaine said. 'Danny asked me not to read it, so I didn't.'

Denise took the paper; opened it up. She recognised

Lily's handwriting. As she started to read she could hear Lily's voice.

Mum calls me a puzzle.
I suppose I am.
I don't do it on purpose
I just don't always know
how to say what's going on.

Instantly the words blurred as Denise's eyes misted over with tears. Impatiently, she brushed them away.

Why can't people understand
without me having to explain?
Why do people need to HEAR what I'm feeling
and why I'm feeling it?
Maybe they're the puzzles,
not me.
Maybe they're puzzles with a piece missing.
The piece that lets them look in my eyes
and know that I'm so scared.

Again Denise wiped her tears.

My mum loved me when it was just me.
But now it's Andy too.
And I don't know if there's enough love
for both of us.

She caught her breath. 'Oh, you silly girl,' she murmured. 'You silly, silly girl. Is that what you think?'

Elaine stood in front of her anxiously. 'What is it, Denise?'

Denise looked up at her but didn't really see her. Clumsily, hastily, she refolded the piece of paper.

'I'm going to get Lily,' she said.

Danny and Rick sat on the garden wall outside the cottage in Bailey Place. Neither of them spoke. They gazed ahead of them with blank expressions, kicked their heels against the brickwork. Denise's car was parked in the road just in front of them.

Inside his head, Danny prayed.

God, please. Please help Lily understand. She thinks I've betrayed her. Let her down. She thinks Rick's betrayed her, too, by bringing me here, but she thinks I'm worse. Loads worse. Because I told her mum where to find her. I gave her mum the poem.

I had to, though, didn't I, God? If Lily's mum didn't know what Lily was feeling, how would she ever understand? You can't make something better if you don't know what's wrong.

I was cross with You when Dad had to go away to work. I'm sorry now, You know I am. And I'll see Dad later because he's coming home for a visit. He'll be back any time now. But a good thing happened because he went away. I met Lily. And maybe I'm the only one Lily would have shown her poem to. Maybe I'm the only one who could let her mum know what Lily's so scared of. That's a very good thing, isn't it?

I still believe it, God. That when we trust You, somehow You work things out for the best. Sometimes we don't like the things You do. Sometimes they hurt. But You love us, so You'll always do what's best for us.

I suppose it's like that with me and Lily. She trusted me

and now she thinks I've let her down. And I know I've hurt her by giving her mum that poem after I promised not to show anyone. But I did it because it was the best thing I could do. It was the only thing I could do. Please, God, please make everything turn out well. Please help Lily to understand. Please help her to forgive me.

Danny's phone bleeped; broke the silence. He read the text and smiled.

'Dad's home.'

Rick glanced at him. 'You'll need to be getting back, then,' he said grimly. He looked behind him at the cottage. 'I wonder how much longer this is going to take?'

Hardly were the words out of his mouth when Lily's mum appeared from round the back of the house. In one hand she carried Lily's bags. Grasped tightly in the other was her daughter's hand. They walked together out to the car.

'Is everything ... all right?' Rick said.

Denise looked at Lily. 'I think so. I hope so.'

Lily looked back at her mum and smiled, as though Rick and Danny weren't there. It was a warm smile, Danny thought. A true smile.

Denise opened the car boot and slung the bags inside. 'Right,' she said. 'Who's in the front with me?'

'Me, please,' said Lily. She crossed in front of Danny without looking at him.

As Denise strapped herself into the driver's seat, she said, 'Thanks for your help, boys. You're more than welcome to come round later if you'd like to, Rick. I've brought something back for you from New Zealand. Just a little thank you for having Lily to stay. And, Danny, you can come round, too, if you'd like to. Don't know what I'd have done without you today.'

Still Lily didn't look at Danny.

'It's really kind,' he mumbled, 'but my dad's just got home from Spain.'

'Has he?' Denise exclaimed. 'I didn't realise! Your mum must be so pleased! What have you got planned for tonight? Anything exciting?'

'Not exciting exactly,' Danny answered. 'I know it sounds stupid but Dad's been watching the moon over in Spain and I've been looking at it over here, and it's been sort of like doing something together. So tonight we're going to stand outside the flat and look at the moon together for real. Side by side.'

Denise smiled. 'It doesn't sound silly at all, Danny. I think it sounds lovely.'

She reached across, picked up Lily's hand and gave it a squeeze. Lily's gaze didn't shift from the window.

But she squeezed back.

It was a clear night. The sky was a deep, dark velvet-blue. Overhead, the moon hung, silent and silver.

Danny stood between his mum and his dad. The three of them gazed upwards, arms wrapped around each other.

'Does the moon look any different from Spain, Dad?' Danny asked.

'Nope,' replied his dad. 'But it looks a whole lot better with you two standing next to me.'

Danny grinned. 'Same.'

His phone bleeped. 'Sorry,' he said. 'I meant to leave it indoors.'

He pulled the mobile out of his pocket; read the text from Lily.

Are u looking at the moon Danny? I am 2. With Mum x

 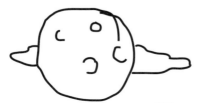

NATIONAL DISTRIBUTORS

UK: (and countries not listed below)

CWR, Waverley Abbey House, Waverley Lane, Farnham, Surrey GU9 8EP.

Tel: (01252) 784700 Outside UK (44) 1252 784700 Email: mail@cwr.org.uk

AUSTRALIA: KI Entertainment, Unit 21 317-321 Woodpark Road, Smithfield, New South Wales 2164.

Tel: 1 800 850 777 Fax: 02 9604 3699 Email: sales@kientertainment.com.au

CANADA: David C Cook Distribution Canada, PO Box 98, 55 Woodslee Avenue, Paris, Ontario N3L 3E5.

Tel: 1800 263 2664 Email: sandi.swanson@davidccook.ca

GHANA: Challenge Enterprises of Ghana, PO Box 5723, Accra.

Tel: (021) 222437/223249 Fax: (021) 226227 Email: ceg@africaonline.com.gh

HONG KONG: Cross Communications Ltd, 1/F, 562A Nathan Road, Kowloon.

Tel: 2780 1188 Fax: 2770 6229 Email: cross@crosshk.com

INDIA: Crystal Communications, 10-3-18/4/1, East Marredpalli, Secunderabad – 500026, Andhra Pradesh.

Tel/Fax: (040) 27737145 Email: crystal_edwj@rediffmail.com

KENYA: Keswick Books and Gifts Ltd, PO Box 10242-00400, Nairobi.

Tel: (020) 2226047/312639 Email: sales.keswick@africaonline.co.ke

MALAYSIA: Canaanland Distributors Sdn Bhd, No. 25 Jalan PJU 1A/41B, NZX Commercial Centre, Ara Jaya, 47301 Petaling Jaya, Selangor.

Tel: (03) 7885 0540/1/2 Fax: (03) 7885 0545 Email: info@canaanland.com.my

Salvation Publishing & Distribution Sdn Bhd, 23 Jalan SS 2/64, 47300 Petaling Jaya, Selangor.

Tel: (03) 78766411/78766797 Fax: (03) 78757066/78756360 Email: info@salvationbookcentre.com

NEW ZEALAND: KI Entertainment, Unit 21 317-321 Woodpark Road, Smithfield, New South Wales 2164, Australia.

Tel: 0 800 850 777 Fax: +612 9604 3699 Email: sales@kientertainment.com.au

NIGERIA: FBFM, Helen Baugh House, 96 St Finbarr's College Road, Akoka, Lagos.

Tel: (+234) 7747429/01-08075201777/08186337699/08154453905 Email: fbfm_1@yahoo.com

PHILIPPINES: OMF Literature Inc, 776 Boni Avenue, Mandaluyong City.

Tel: (02) 531 2183 Fax: (02) 531 1960 Email: gloadlaon@omflit.com

SINGAPORE: Alby Commercial Enterprises Pte Ltd, 95 Kallang Avenue #04-00, AIS Industrial Building, 339420.

Tel: (65) 629 27238 Fax: (65) 629 27235 Email: marketing@alby.com.sg

SRI LANKA: Christombu Publications (Pvt) Ltd, Bartleet House, 65 Braybrooke Place, Colombo 2.

Tel: (9411) 2421073/2447665 Email: christombupublications@gmail.com

USA: David C Cook Distribution Canada, PO Box 98, 55 Woodslee Avenue, Paris, Ontario N3L 3E5, Canada.

Tel: 1800 263 2664 Email: sandi.swanson@davidccook.ca

CWR is a Registered Charity – Number 294387

CWR is a Limited Company registered in England – Registration Number 1990308

More Topz SECRET STORIES!

Why not try the others in the series?

The *Topz Secret Stories* are full of fun and they also help you to discover things about yourself and God. The Dixons Gang present problems and opportunities to the Topz Gang.

The Cloudgate Mystery
ISBN: 978-1-85345-992-4

For an art project, Clyde from the Dixons Gang creates a mysterious piece he calls 'The Cloudgate'. But when no one understands, he feels like giving up. The Topz Gang help to persuade Clyde that he has real talent and that regardless of what other people may think, all our efforts matter to God.

One Too Many For Benny
ISBN: 978-1-85345-915-3
Pantomime Pandemonium
ISBN: 978-1-85345-916-0
Dixons' Den
ISBN: 978-1-85345-690-9
Dixons and the Wolf
ISBN: 978-1-85345-691-6

For current prices, visit **www.cwr.org.uk/store**
Available online or from Christian bookshops.

Topz Secret Diaries

These *Topz Secret Diaries* will help you discover things about yourself and God. Includes questions and quizzes, engaging puzzles, word searches, doodles, lists to write and more.

Boys Only
ISBN: 978-1-85345-596-4
126page paperback,
197x129mm

Just for Girls
ISBN: 978-1-85345-597-1
126page paperback,
197x129mm

Benny's Barmy Bits
ISBN: 978-1-85345-431-8

Danny's Daring Days
ISBN: 978-1-85345-502-5

Dave's Dizzy Doodles
ISBN: 978-1-85345-552-0

**Gruff & Saucy's
Topzy-Turvy Tales**
ISBN: 978-1-85345-553-7

John's Jam-Packed Jottings
ISBN: 978-1-85345-503-2

Josie's Jazzy Journal
ISBN: 978-1-85345-457-8

Paul's Potty Pages
ISBN: 978-1-85345-456-1

Sarah's Secret Scribblings
ISBN: 978-1-85345-432-5

Topz is a colourful daily devotional just for you

In each issue the Topz Gang teach children biblical truths through word games, puzzles, riddles, cartoons, competitions, simple prayers and daily Bible readings.

Available as an annual subscription or as single issues.

For current prices or to purchase any of the above titles go to **www.cwr.org.uk/store** call 01252 784700 or visit a Christian bookshop.